KOWLOON WALLED CITY, 1984

BY

NICHOLAS MORINE

ISBN-13: 978-1-927996-06-5

Published by Problematic Press.

To purchase copies of this book, please visit:
http://problematicpress.wordpress.com

Printed in the United States.

Cover design by Nicholas Morine.

The hat logo is a trademark of Problematic Press.

To all those who dwell in communities that once were and are no longer.

To warriors, young and old, who fight their battles with limitless courage. To Dorian Murray (#Dstrong).

To my family and friends – those that have never left my side no matter how ill the weather.

CONTENTS

CHAPTER 1:

HAK NAM

Water ran down the broken concrete walls in a constant stream, rain mixed with filth. A skinny young man with a rolled smoke hanging loosely from his lips wheeled a makeshift barrow down the darkened avenues, along the line of Lo Yan street that cut the city in two from North to South. The barrow was heavy with bags of flour, marked with elegant script. The youth wheeling the cart was destined for Yeung's Noodle Shop, a one-room affair that doubled as the family bedroom and kitchen. Deep creases were worn into the rough stone streets, which were narrow and claustrophobic. Thin bars of sickly light cast their faces down upon those on the thoroughfare. A bent, elderly woman with spiderweb hair wrapped loosely in a brown bandana, gripped her cane and leaned against the wall for support. She stopped, heaving, and reached into the many folds of her threadbare pants, pulling forth a battered cigarette container.

He passed by, wrists starting to burn slightly from the exertion of holding the heavy cart upright and in place. The cheap metal wheel clanged noisily against its brackets, wobbling as he drove it forward down Lo Yan.

Rough-cut entrances with hand painted signage spoke to him on either side. He passed by doctor's offices, curiosity corners, and scrap metal shops. Wires, loosely bundled together with bits of steel or twine, ran above, nestled next to dew dropped pipes. The earthy and primitive smell of the damp permeated the air, inescapable, though it faded as the days passed and one became used to it until it melted into the milieu. The black mould was everywhere. Irregular veins of the stuff shot through pitted concrete, rotten wood, and rusted metal.

The soft rubber of the wheel strained under the weight of the wheelbarrow, as did the youth's aching wrists. He took another pull at his rollie, feeling the cherry inch towards him, rolling paper curling and flaking away into ash. Smoke filled his mouth, throat, and lungs with a familiar stinging warmth. He exhaled a plume and felt the tingle of strength return to his fingers. His legs pressed forward, and the patched and worn wheel gave way as it crawled along its muddy rut.

He reached Yeung's after a moment, hearing the excited yells of a mob echoing from the outside, at the terminus of Lo Yan, where the sun first touched the foot of the city. The young man paused a moment at the threshold of the noodle shop, conflicted by the rising excitement in his blood and the sweet scent of spice and fresh pasta that called to his empty stomach.

"Don't just darken the damned door, get in here!" hollered Mr. Yeung, the eponymous proprietor of the noodle shop. He was bent low over a flour-encrusted cutting board, working dumplings. In recent years Yeung's Noodle Shop had made a name for itself inside the Walled City, and even a few discerning neighbourhoods outside.

Bo did as his boss said, cutting the cart a sharp right and pushing it into the tiny "warehouse" – in reality, a spare corner of the one-room operation. A few stacks of flour bearing the same proud red and black lettering were strewn in this corner, white powder over cracked vinyl tile.

"You're late as hell!" Yeung fumed, his already red cheeks darkening plum, contrasting the spider-like veins that crawled through his skin.

"Sorry, Mr. Yeung." Bo made a perfunctory bow at the waist, never lowering his eyes. The old man hated weaklings; it was best to show some spine even in shame. He butted the smoke out against the wall and tossed the spent filter away into some nearby rubbish.

"That's better! A little appreciation around here!" the old man harrumphed from under his push-broom moustache, salt and pepper and picked bare in spots. He took his eyes from the heavy cart and the tired boy pushing it, returning his gaze to the cutting board in front of him, his hands working mechanically.

"There's a lot of noise going on outside."

"Who cares?" Yeung groused. "Your work is inside." He finished another dumpling and then shimmied a few steps to the left to grab a wok full of steaming spiced pork for the filled variety. With the same steps, he moved back to his prep area, a few loose strands of white hair falling loose from his bandana.

"I've been working a lot lately."

"Work is life. Life is work. You were born here. You should know that."

"I'm going out there to see." Yeung's dismissive attitude burned at the boy's pride. Bo ground his teeth and began to stack the heavy bags on top of each other on the floor.

"Yes. Yes. After you finish the job."

The next ten minutes were spent sweating. Bo's back bent low as he laid the sacks down, lifting them with trembling arms from the barrow. He was not a very large boy for thirteen and grit often stood in place of strength. Mr. Yeung whistled a tune as he poked pork into the center of his locally famous delicacies. The spices were a family secret, and Bo was decidedly not family, merely the paid help. It was probably the same cheap mix the rest of the shops used, despite how loudly Yeung might protest, proclaiming his to possess true flavour. Bo liked the pork-filled dumplings the best, loving the taste of the meat which would fill his stomach for hours.

Before Bo stood tall stacks of flour, as even as could be managed given the load. The boy stood with arms on his hips, chest heaving as he took deep breaths of the moist air thick with ginger and pepper. Yeung took a moment's attention away from his handiwork, turning his thick torso to face the boy. Sausage-like fingers encrusted in flour beat at the front of a homemade apron.

"Not bad Bo-boy. You're getting quicker."

Bo accepted this praise in silence, knowing it better to say nothing.

"The stacks are neater, too. I think you're finally learning," Yeung said.

Bo had been working for Mr. Yeung now for nearly a year. This sort of compliment was rare, and so he bowed his head slightly. What came next was completely unexpected. With some sleight of hand or small magic, Yeung showed a handful of brown coin. Bo quickly counted $10 in $1s and $2s. The Queen was engraved on one side, Hong Kong's coat of arms on the other – no room for Kowloon Walled City. For the first time in weeks, Bo saw Yeung smile, the sour expression fleeing from his face. The noodle man's flushed cheeks gave him a comical appearance as he pushed his hand forward.

"You deserve it. You have never let me down."

Bo was bad at taking compliments and cast his eyes to the floor, burning hot with the threat of tears.

"Except for being late a few times," Yeung finished with a smirk. Bo chuckled despite himself and brought his head up. He felt the warm coins being pressed into his hand.

"Go. Play."

The older man dismissed the boy with a parting crack about the shoulders, leaving a flour hand-print.

Bo didn't have to be told twice, turning on his heel and navigating his way adeptly about the buckets and pans strewn about the shop as he left. Yeung was left alone with his thoughts. Seeing the young boy fly away from him, he thought of the letter he'd received earlier in the week, stamped with a government seal. The offer they were making to shut down his business here in the walled city and to relocate somewhere else in Kowloon – subject to all of the proper scrutiny and regulations, of course – was substantial. Would Bo come with him? Would the boy even want to leave his home, the place he was born? Yeung sighed, buried his anxiety, and returned to work, hands setting to making more dough for dumplings.

Bo sprinted through the door frame and heard the sound of shouting – from outside.

To his right was the end of Lo Yan. Now there was a steady stream of people moving past him, headed towards the clamour. Most were young men, a few women, and a few teens like himself, running between legs and tripping up slowpokes. A few old men tottered along at the margins, either sporting long beards whitened with age or clean shaven, resembling spotted gargoyles. All carried umbrellas, factory-made or makeshift, grey water sluicing down the thin fabric and pooling in the muddy grit at their feet. Some carried small bags or rode rusting bicycles, twisting the handlebars so that they didn't fall over.

Having no cover of his own, Bo nipped at the heels of the human crush. Still, wetness dappled his hair and chilled his nape. The shouts and screams became louder, surrounding him as the crowd broke outside, spilling free. The night sky was obliterated by a ring of bright halogen lights; a semi-circle of mottled cars and trucks pushed their hi-beams up against the northern exterior of the walled city. Bo had to raise a hand to cover his eyes, shielding them from the light as his vision adjusted. Behind the cars, bright eyed and laughing like hyenas, thugs intoxicated on beer and bloodlust hooted, some calling out for betting sheets. Bo felt rough hands pressing into his back, urging him forward. He stumbled a bit before catching himself.

The din was drowned out by a behemoth noise, a roar that rumbled the very ground beneath Bo's feet. The thin material of his shoes transmitted the familiar tremors; he craned his neck to look upward. The lamps on the wings and underbelly of the jetliner were like shooting stars attached to a trailing grey mass, flying so close to the walled city he always felt he could reach out and rub the chassis like a contented alley cat.

The passenger jet shot over the rooftop and began the rest of its descent into Kai Tak Airport on the west side of the bay. The blue water of Kowloon Bay was one of Bo's favourite memories, a place he'd gone with his parents when they were still alive. The port sidled up to the bay was dangerous – industrial. And, you weren't supposed to be there... not that it mattered. He never left the city anymore.

As the screaming engines faded away, the excited cries of the mob returned in greater measure. Bo nipped and tucked his way in between the tangles of limbs, navigating his way shoulder first to part the tide of flesh. He heard the loud thump of dance music, synth pad drums beating their way out of a sound system. Had to be Hane, a Japanese on the run and community character, one of the few that traversed the city and the outside at will, coming and going as he pleased. Bo envied him, finally breaking through the perimeter of the crowd and catching a few filthy looks, seeking the source of the music.

He saw Hane atop the hood of his car, a tricked out American Mustang, glossy midnight black. He was vibrating with energy, pumping his fist in the air, bright red leather jacket flying like a banner. His bleached blonde hair was spiked up – his signature look. Then Bo saw the source of the evening's excitement.

Two men, shirtless and covered in battle-scars, circled one another with fists raised and eyes afire. One was a very young man, short and lean, his hair jet black and wild, a face marred by a broken nose that had been poorly reset. His only other distinguishing feature aside from this was a long white scar running the length of his left forearm, ugly and ragged.

The other fighter was a man approaching middle years, much larger than his youthful opponent, thick and muscular and hirsute, an unkempt beard spread across his wide and wrinkled face. Both men moved with purpose and martial techniques familiar to many in attendance.

The bright hi-beams of the ring of rusted vehicles painted the fighters in stark relief, casting their long shadows like an ancient play upon the uneven balconies of the south-facing city facade. Their dark sides stalked one another. They sized up one another; the larger man was grinning at the young man like prey – the young man expressionless yet intent, focused. The open air accommodated the cacophony of the crowd, allowed the thumping bass from Hane's tricked ride to expand out against the concrete. Hane had gently hopped off the hood of his Mustang and was now rolling a smoke absently, looking down to his lap. The humidity of late summer laid a thick sweat on them all, a light rain collecting in everyone's hair and dripping from the arrays of aerials lining the top of the walled city like barbed wire. The water was cooling now as the sun had been missing from the sky for some time.

Bo recognized the older man. Li Zhao. Not new to the sport, Li Zhao was a fading legend in the City. He had been said to have slowed down in recent years, but Bo saw no hesitation in his step, nor slack in his physique despite his age. The young man was much smaller and more compact, nondescript. He looked like a nobody if there ever was one, and the odds reflected his poor chances. The board hastily mounted on a nearby truckbed showed Li Zhao at 8:1. Yet, Bo had the distinct feeling he had seen the challenger fight before, and win. Fang Shi was his name, scrawled hastily on the board below Li Zhao.

Li's animal grace seemed to reflect the confidence of the house bookkeepers; by contrast his smaller and more youthful opponent moved with what seemed to be restrained agitation, the pacing of a caged tiger.

Li suddenly broke the fluidity of his forms, having masked his eyes and facial features from emotion, striking snakelike with a jab which caught the smaller man across the face, spinning him about. The crowd laughed, seeing Fang clutch at his nose while looking up through a mop of hair was a comical image. If the young man heard the jeering, he paid little mind, pulling his hands free to reveal a bloody nose, almost certainly broken – again. He returned to his fighting stance, circling and prowling. Fury shone in his eyes.

Li raised his arms, showboating, before launching a flurry of advancing kicks, fast and straight. Bo could barely make out the blur that was his legs as he moved through the air. Fang was faster however, managing to sidestep the attack and driving a crushing elbow to the back of Li's head. The old man staggered, his forward momentum carrying him into an awkward roll – more like a fall. The rules of this particular bout dictated that a man be allowed to regain his feet, and so the young man with the broken nose stood stock still. Fang regarded his opponent coolly, as if from a distance even though he was a touch away. Li Zhao stumbled to his feet, shaking his head all the while. Blood crawled from a cut on his lip, road rash from the pavement underfoot.

The men surrounding Bo on either side were wild-eyed. Feral grins split their faces. Even those conservative gamblers holding red tickets for Li Zhao seemed to be enflamed with passion despite the potential loss of their wager, their worn rags flapping in the evening wind as they shadowboxed, throwing catcalls and empty threats. What had been a distraction on the undercard had become something to *see*, a new story that would be whispered inside the walled city for all the days to come. Bo felt himself rising along with them, on the edge of the tide, pumping his small fist in the air and giving a warrior's cry as the two men rushed at one another.

Hane cranked the volume dial and let his subwoofers boom. Smoke curled out above deep-tinted windows.

The unknown fighter led the offensive, a spinning back kick that failed to connect followed up with a vicious elbow that Li Zhao blocked just before it took his head off.

Counterpunching, the older man pulled a trick he'd learned from a fight years ago, going above his opponent's guard, bringing his knuckles hard across Fang's face. Fang toppled over, eyes rolling up into the back of his head, all in an instant.

Bo thought the fight was over, seeing the young man fall back and land square on his ass, a shocked look on his face. His nose was pouring crimson now, turned at a grotesque angle. Blood streamed like a small river down across his chin, dripping like rain onto his chest.

Then Fang rolled over to take a knee, attempting to stand. His eyes were dull and stupid. He was panting with exhaustion.

"Get up! Get up!" the chanting began. Bo joined in enthusiastically.

Fang pushed himself from his knees with shaking arms and legs, swaying slightly as he fought to raise his guard. Shaking his head with disapproval at having to shame his opponent, Li Zhao's face took on a grim cast as he once again pressed forward, fists at the ready to finish the fight. Almost faster than the eye could see, the light returned to the youth's eyes, as a star hidden behind a cloud for but a moment. His stance dropped low, his guard firmed in the blink of an eye. Li Zhao did not have time to express his surprise, moving with his own expertise to block the spinning back-fist he saw coming in his mind's eye.

I won't be fooled by the same trick twice, boy.

The back-fist never came. The underdog had swept Li's leg with incredible speed, snapping his hips about for maximum leverage, slicing Li off at the knee and spinning him hard to the pavement. The finisher elicited simultaneous gasps and cheers from the crowd, burying the sickening thud of a human skull striking concrete. Li Zhao felt the world violently tilt out from under him before curtains of pain shuttered his consciousness.

Several long seconds followed. The spectators fell silent. Only the music remained – and even that was fading as Hane turned down the dial. They were listening for Li and listening to the ragged breathing of the only man left standing, the unknown fighter with the badge of blood on his breast, the man who had been fighting for some time in obscurity to even cinch this chance against the legendary Li.

This total reversal of fortune cemented the fight as historic, engraved into the mythology of the walled city. A fan favourite had been defeated in heroic and unexpected fashion by a complete newcomer to the circuit.

The doctor scurrying to the downed Li Zhao was scarcely noticed as a new people's champion was crowned for the night. A mad mob rushed forward to embrace their new hero, to lift him onto their shoulders. Bo was nearly trampled by the stampede, but he was practiced enough in navigating through crowds and small spaces to dodge serious hurt as hundreds of people milled past him, pushing forward in a crush.

"FANG! FANG! FANG!"

Eyes had swept over the betting sheets for a second time, catching the new champion's name and throwing it to the wind, that it might hold it and carry his glory. A thousand voices and fists thrust into the night sky, reverberating from the walls of the city. Hundreds more souls joined in from sagging balconies, excited children poking their small faces between rusted rungs.

Bo had to retreat from the front, being crushed on all sides by much larger men, rioting with abandon. He managed to turn, looking back as he shouldered his way against the tide. A hundred hungry hands lifted the bruised flesh of their new hero up into the fluorescent parking lights.

CHAPTER 2:

WATER

The water ran down his back, warm, stinging with soap. The moisture sought his wounds and swept over and into them. A soft dark cloth stroked the length of his spine, across his ribs, washing clotted blood away in streaks before a second stroke made them disappear into the rag.

Small hands wrung the cloth, the dirty water dripping the colour of rust into a basin below. A reedy voice, low and urgent, worried: "Fang Shi. What am I thinking, dating you?!"

He chose not to reply. A lit cigarette hung from his lip – one from a pack this time instead of the usual loose roll. His winnings were heavy in his pocket, warm coins pressing into his thigh. He blew a thick plume of smoke and took a deep breath, feeling his lungs stutter.

"You know that my father will see you like this. He will know."

Yeah. Fang knew that her father would find out, likely before noon. If he didn't see the marks on Fang's face, he'd hear through the exchange, through the passing of gossip. Confirmation would take no longer than an instant; Fang could see a striking mental image of Fu Ren, his broad, stern face set in stony disapproval. Fang didn't give a shit, but thought better of saying so.

He heard Lin move around him, seated on a low bench in a stall next to the main faucet. Private and very inexpensive, they'd paid only a few dollars for the privilege of a box, a bench, and a ratty curtain hatched in a bright pink and yellow. The air was wet and carried the tar-pepper taste of spores. Black continents sprawled across the cracked tile walls, beaded and perspiring. Lin wrinkled her nose as she sat lightly, tending to his injuries. Lin Ren looked at him with eyes the colour of expensive chocolates, the sweets he saw behind glass on his runs outside the walls. He smiled despite his pride, cigarette bobbing, dropping ash from the cherry on top of his boots.

"And you simply don't care, do you?" she laughed, seeing his wolfish smile. Her heart

23

saw his for a moment and held it there. Fang shook his head, eyes bloodshot, looking barbaric with mats in his jet black mane. The smile in her eyes retreated, irises contracting like a snake before it strikes.

"Well you damned well should," she hissed, drawing near and cupping her hands firmly about the base of his broken nose.

There is a sharp and sudden twist. A pop and lock reset the joint. Cartilage snapped, and a sword of pain drove through Fang's mind, like being smashed hard with a stone. He gasped and squeezed his eyelids shut, wetness springing forth and rolling down his cheeks betraying his suffering.

Then, it was over.

Lin's soft hands held his head gently, her fingers massaging him through his hair, thick with sweat. His body was shuddering, heaving, the definition of tension and release. He felt her lips at his temple, pressing gently, cooling him, reassuring and sensual.

"And you tell me you won tonight?" she whispered to him, taunting.

"You tell me," he guided her hand to the mass of coins in his pocket. His arms were still shaking.

"Is that supposed to impress me? I like your face better without the blood and the swelling."

She withdrew her hand from his grip. Taunting turned to point.

"It should. Tonight I dropped a legend. And became one myself. And earned more in one night than I have in the last year."

"Anything else, Fang? Or have you traded your mind for a broken nose and a few dollars?"

The fighter snatched the cigarette away from his mouth and exhaled with a clear note of agitation.

"It's not like that. It's not like that." The smoke curled away as he rested his scarred forearm on his knee, still twitching.

"It is. This is the second time we've had to do this." Lin held up pale hands coloured scarlet. "You promised me you weren't going to get hurt."

"Not as hurt as the other guy."

"A quick joke and an easy smile don't impress me as much as they used to, Fang Shi."

"Okay. So I was wrong about a few things. They gave me the champ right away. That's not how it was supposed to be."

Lin walked around him. He heard the sound of water moving about the basin as she washed her hands clean of him.

"I am not a fool, Fang. I know that you don't

plan to stop fighting. Even if you lied to me and told me you would never get hurt, and that you would only do it once. I lied to myself because I saw through you and I'm still here."

He smiled and pulled the cigarette from his lips, shushing her with his other finger. Her voice was carrying well above the open ceiling of the stall. Lin shot a frustrated look at him and said nothing, crossing her arms in critical repose. Despite the late hour she looked as beautiful as ever to Fang, the soft pastels of her sweater standing out against the drab walls of the city. Her cuffs were rolled back to the elbow. None of his blood remained on her hands. They were soft and small and very fair.

"How much money?"

"More than enough to take you out. Dinner and a movie?"

Lin didn't blush nor skip a beat.

"I asked you how much money. Save the sweet talk until after I'm satisfied with your answers."

Fang shook his head.

"Then forget about the date."

"Five thousand."

Her eyebrows lifted in surprise.

"Still mad at me?"

"Yes. Just a little less."

"Nice to know my life has a price."

Lin smirked, mirroring his cynicism.

"Everyone's does. Besides, as long as they stick to breaking your nose instead of the rest of your face..."

She leaned in and kissed him, hungrily. There was the slight taste of iron mixed with her fresh, almost floral scent. It was intoxicating. Fang reached for her, wrapping his arms around her waist, pulling her onto his lap. The muscles of his legs were tender and he gasped as he did so.

"Poor baby," she cooed.

Again they tasted one another, desperate in their need for one another. Their hands slid over each others' bodies, feeling soft flesh and hard muscle. After a moment, the lovers sank apart, sighing.

It was not the right time or place. The stench of the mildew intruded. Fang's nose was swelling at an incredible rate and hurt, throbbing. Their time was almost up – it was dangerous for Lin to be caught leaving her apartment at this hour of the night, now nearing morning. The only way to tell was an increasing buzz of human activity about them – the sound, the bustle. The sun was obscured to them here in the heart of the labyrinth. A bare light bulb hanging from a wire swung in lazy circles above them.

"I have to go." He said it first.

"Me too. My father is starting to suspect my absences."

"So? You're old enough to do whatever you want now."

"It's not that simple Fang."

She left his lap and stood, straightening her clothes and hair. He joined her, embracing her, feeling her heat against him.

"One kiss for the road, hey?" she said. Their lips met briefly and they smiled into each other, passion mirrored in their eyes.

Trailing her fingers down his side, Lin turned and left the stall, pushing the curtains aside and stepping out into the pump room before disappearing. Fang brought the back of his hand to his lips, his tongue darting out and still tasting notes of her. He closed his eyes for a moment's peace, recalling her face to mind. He smiled to himself as more footsteps could be heard moving back and forth in front of his cubicle.

He stepped out into the pump room, now filling with tired looking people gripping battered plastic jugs and buckets. Old men with leather faces stood impassively, joints creaking in the morning humidity, sniffing and coughing phlegm. Bent women scooped up idle, cranky toddlers, herding them, trying to keep them in the line. One young boy in particular he caught staring at him quizzically, eyes slitted and squinting.

"Help you, kid?" Fang called as he left his stall, making his way past the line and toward Kwong Ming street, or "bright street". He was hoping to see a little sunlight today before work. The boy did not shy away, merely straightening up and holding his gaze. Probably saw the fight last night, Fang reasoned, feeling prideful. He puffed out his chest slightly as he exited the pump room, entering the flow of morning foot-traffic down Kwong Ming.

Mailboxes peppered the depleted walls of the avenue, fire engine red and emerald green with white lettering. Drooping, discoloured envelopes and handbills lolled like wagging tongues tugged by the breeze of those passing by. The air became gradually fresher as he walked, staring at the back of bobbing heads. A small promise of the coming dawn stretched through the wires and pipework, splashing against the stone siding in a length of a few metres. On either side there were small and packed cafes, coffee and cigarettes being exchanged under the awnings – standing room only. The chairs were stacked high in a corner to the side, ready to be brought out after the morning rush. Several squatters lounged in the rising sunlight, low with their backs against the wall, almost flattened. The rest walked on slowly, envious.

The sunlight felt warm on his skin; a chill thrilled through his spine. His skin, gooseflesh, rustled against his soiled clothes. He shrugged his shoulders and allowed his head to hang, allowing the warmth to coat the narrow angle of his shoulders.

Then he was through the narrows and back in the shade. Taking a quick left turn, and then a right, he passed by his favourite take-out. Fang fought the urge to stop for some rice and beef, feeling very hungry but fearing being too late. Thick steam billowed up from the cooking pans and carried notes of savoury herbs to him, wafting down the corridor as he approached the strip, and causing him to doubt his decision to press on.

Heroin Strip opened up to Fang, double wide, triple wide in places. The usual clotheslines bearing limp shirts and ragged pants were absent, replaced by crisscrossing lines bearing lanterns of every shade. Most remained lit, shining through their flimsy painted paper housings. They were the only light, the sun never showing its face here. Makeshift tables lined the walls in irregular fashion, some draped and canopied stalls and booths among them. Behind each, a salesman or saleswoman, from eight to eighty years old. He started walking down the ramp into the strip, the smell of incense and tobacco smoke mingling with the scent of spices and cooked meat, masking less pleasant odours. The perpetual darkness eased the eyes of the addicts that slept here in the early hours and moped about during the rest of the day, constant customers.

Fang recognized more than half of them at a glance, his steps taking him past a few curled and wretched souls. Some tugged at rotten blankets while others pulled at their hair or their skin, anxious and cold. He walked past them, keeping his eyes moving, alert for any sign of trouble.

His stall was near the far end, where Heroin Strip spilled out over into the Dens. Larger and more amenable apartments for the bosses. There was only one way in or out of the Dens, and that was through this small but lengthy strip. This allowed plenty of time to evade the authorities should they ever come calling. They almost never did. Fang corrected himself; nowadays – they came at least once a month. Things were changing around here. The wasted bodies huddled up against the walls and skulking in the shadows with needles in their arms were not the only ones who felt fear.

A rack of sizzling bacon being cooked up on an electric griddle caught his attention for a moment. Fang realized he could no longer escape his hunger. He had a soft spot for Western bacon, and due to a few expatriates living in the Walled City, he was able to indulge himself every once in a while. The salt and the cured smoke of the meat and familiar warmth of the fried eggs were a private and personal pleasure. He stopped and eyed the squat American woman he'd come to know quite well over the years.

"Knew you couldn't just walk on by!" Viola called to him, devilry in her small brown eyes.

"Couldn't. Smelled the bacon," Fang said. His English was far from perfect, but practice with the cook and a few other Westerners he worked with had made his handle of the language workable.

"Funny thing that. I should really get a fume hood to take that nasty smell away from here!"

Fang smiled good-naturedly.

"Do that and I'll have to get serious."

A flicker of fear crossed the elderly

woman's face, creasing line upon worry-line. It passed as swiftly as it had come.

"You wouldn't dare!" she said. "Who would keep that belly full without me here?"

Fang laughed, pulling a few larger coins from his pocket and palming them softly onto the scratched wooden table, next to the grill.

"Hungry boy, eh?"

"You know it. Full breakfast, please. Extra bacon."

All business, Viola nodded and set to it, spooning up a handful of fried potatoes, two fried eggs, and eight rashers of bacon. She neatly passed the paper plate to Fang and then counted his coins.

"You gave me too much – a few dollars extra."

"Keep it. Your food is the best."

She smiled back at his praise as he nodded awkwardly, turning away back into foot traffic as he picked at the potatoes with bare hands. The spices were just right, as always, and the food very fresh. He never felt cheated of his money when he dealt with Viola. That was something that could not be said of all of the dealers here on the strip, let alone the rest of the walled city. He had nearly finished his meal, savouring the salty crunch of the bacon, as he arrived at his stall for the day's work.

Yu looked up at him, slightly amused, his square jaw moving rhythmically at the chewing tobacco. He hawked and spat on the ground by his stool and shot a glance at Fang's plate.

"Gah! Damn freak meat again, Fang?"

"You haven't lived until you've tried Viola's bacon, Yu."

"Smoked and salt pork is nothing special. I eat it all the time. My favourite comes with the rind, too. What makes hers so great?"

"It's a whole different thing Yu. Here, try a piece."

Fang leaned over the table, pinching a piece of perfectly done, fatty bacon. Yu snatched it from his fingers and tossed it into his mouth, chewing at it.

"Hmmm..."

"Well?"

"Yeah. It's pretty fuckin' good. Probably great with egg and ramen."

Their table was long, in a prominent place. The brown paper packets lined up in eye-catching arrangements held the heroin that he was supposed to guard, and sometimes help to sell. Yu Cheng was his partner and the primary salesman. They worked for the 14K. Both of them held the rank of 49er, front-line soldiers. Yu was a talker, and Fang provided a bit of discretionary muscle if the situation called for it. Fanned out like a deck of cards atop a magician's table, the packets held enough for a day's supply to the average addict. Cheap and convenient, their stall did a great deal of business. Their regulars collapsed against soggy cardboard boxes or wooden pallets nearby, at the margins of the strip, as they rigged up the hit. It was fairly early in the morning and Fang only recognized one of the newer customers lazing against the wall to the left, eyes glassy.

"You makin' time with the Ren girl again? What's her name…"

"You know her name, don't play stupid with me, Yu." Fang dropped into a mock fighting stance, holding his steaming plate with overacted grace. A sly smile spread across his lips and a playful light entered his eyes. Yu laughed, slopping his bowl of soup over the side of the ceramic bowl in his hands.

"Ow! Ouch! Damn!" he passed the bowl to one hand and wiped at the side with the front of his shirt, a dull brown affair.

"Serves you right."

"Give me a break, man! I was just making conversation!"

"Stick to eating. Better and safer for both

of us."

Yu scowled back at his gang brother playfully, soon dipping his chopsticks back into the bowl, hunting for stray bits of pork.

"You still didn't answer me about Lin."

"Yeah, I just saw her. Want to make somethin' of it?" Fang bristled slightly.

"Easy! Easy! It's not exactly a secret, Fang. Nothing new. Not your usual." A leer crept across Yu's wide face.

"Keep it to yourself. We're on the job."

"So serious. Also not your usual." The curl of Yu's lip remained in place, cresting his stained teeth. He'd been in the gang longer than Fang had. Rank had privileges, even if they technically occupied the same position.

"You had your goddamn coffee yet? Doesn't seem like it," Fang retorted.

Yu kept the grin static on his face as he slowly reached behind his makeshift chair, fumbling for the cup sitting on the lip of the pallet behind them both. He brought it forth with a flourish.

"Got everything covered, big man," joked Yu, with emphasis on this last. Yu was larger than Fang by half, but had obviously heard the whispers, the stories echoing quickly throughout the walled city.

Fang moved around the tabletop displaying their wares and started to build his own seat next to his partner. He dragged the wire cage from its familiar spot behind the empty bottles – knocking a few down in the process with a tinkling clatter – and shook the water from the rusted lower rungs. A pool of fetid water and stale beer ran in a trickle towards where their stall met the inner wall.

Their first customer of the day approached. He was wearing a too-large leather jacket, torn in a few places and fixed with hand-stitching. He was a regular. Chan.

"How's it going, Chan?" Fang opened.

"Not bad. Wish your boys wouldn't be so loud when they're roughing up a mark. Couldn't get a shit's worth of sleep last night over all the noise some of those rats was making." The dull-eyed man in the leather jacket nonchalantly tossed a few bills on the table; enough for two packets.

Yu laughed, scooping up the small envelopes of heroin in his free hand while the other idly placed his bowl on the seat.

"Big spender today, hey? Sorry to keep you up all night Chan, but debts are debts. And we don't fuck around."

A quick beat passed before Chan's addled mind could reply – Fang cut in.

"... and it's good for business, apparently."

Chan caught up, his confused expression

turning to a lighter favour, chuckling to himself and shaking his head from side to side. Long strands of dirty hair waved as he did so.

"Yeah. Good for business. Don't really care as long as you boys are still here tomorrow and the parlour stays open."

Now it was Fang's turn to be friendly, showing the slightest hint of his true smile.

"You know we'll take care of you, Chan. Anyone gives you shit, you come to us, you know?"

Chan nodded, inclining his head, still laughing to himself over the small joke. He had snatched the heroin from Yu's hands with the skill of a card shark, spiriting them away in the various zipped compartments of his trademark jacket as reflex, almost unnoticed.

"... Oh yeah. And never short us. Steal from us. That's the other side of the Tao. The teachings. Tell the rats, if you see them," Fang said coolly.

Chan bowed, his Adam's apple taking a deep dive as he did so, hands trembling slightly, backing away. The haggard addict backed with an almost supernatural grace into the flow of human traffic, floating away, gone from their sight.

"Getting hard now, are ya?" Yu shuffled on his feet lazily, craning his neck to look at

Fang's face.

"Just making sure he doesn't get fast with us. Or think we're weak," Fang rasped.

"Talk like that can be bad for business."

"I don't think so. Drugs sell. Being nice only makes you soft. And dead."

The matter was settled at that, and Yu set down heavily, spilling his broth and noodles onto the concrete. The bowl broke, shattering on impact, pasta and pork strewn lazily across the pieces.

Yu cursed using every filthy word in his vocabulary. It was more creative than Fang would have imagined; the fighter sat back and crossed his arms with a bemused expression as he watched his friend hover over the lost meal.

The day passed uneventfully, almost mundane. The milling crowds pressed up against them during the noontime rush, the afternoon fix, the steady stream that was the evening gambol. Bills and envelopes changed hands like the wind that never dared to touch the strip, avoiding it like a fell and stagnant pit.

CHAPTER 3:
PATIENTS
AND PRACTICE

Dr. Ren held the delicate steel instruments in his hands. His fingers wrapped around them, thin beige gloves crinkling and creaking against the textured grips. A small radio with a faux-chrome finish buzzed away, sitting next to his instrument tray. A flickering fluorescent light in the far corner of the office gave most patients a headache; Ren advised them to shut their eyes and simply let go, listening to the sound of strings and light singing as he worked.

A few mirrors hung from the walls on taut wire. Certificates from decades ago hung beside them, the paper curling at the corners and stained tobacco brown. A chipped plastic countertop ran a narrow ledge across the periphery of the room at about waist height – well kept, a few objects placed upon it with meticulous care. A fresh lily with baby's breath was arranged artfully in a simple blue vase. There was a brass figurine of two workhorses pulling at the yoke, a rural-looking fisherman bouncing on the buckboard. In a far corner, a red candle burned down halfway, wax tumbling over the sides and pooling around the base. The wick was blackened, trimmed short.

"Looks like you're going to need that tooth pulled. It's infected," Ren said through his cotton face mask, tied tight against his jaw. His voice was barely above a whisper.

"Yeah, yeah. It hurts like hell."

"I can see that." Ren pressed the mirror against the back of the man's gumline to get a better look. "If I don't extract that tooth right now you could be in serious trouble."

The patient attempted laughter, his potbelly shaking up and down in the chair, the noise coming out strangled. Ren took the mirror out of the man's mouth.

"I can do it." Ren reached toward the table for his bottle of brandy. "Want a slug?"

The man nodded and strained to sit up in his chair. Ren poured the amber liquid into a small plastic cup and passed it to his patient.

Best way to keep repeat customers over the years, he'd found, was to keep them drunk. The patient was middle-aged, with a face that seemed friendly and eager to please. A slight moustache graced his upper lip. He downed the small glass in one go.

"Another? I can't give you more than that or you might bleed too much." His hand was still around the handle of the liquor.

The stocky man in the chair shifted, nodding. Ren poured another generous shot for his patient, a Mr. Bolo. He'd signed the ledger on the way in with stubby fingers gripping the pencil, name just barely legible.

"Ready?"

Mr. Bolo simply turned large, liquid eyes on Fu Ren, the oldest practicing dentist in the city, and nodded.

The patient didn't even scream as the metal cut into his gum line.

An hour later, Dr. Ren sat in the same chair, elbows on the armrest, cradling a tumbler of brandy and ice in one hand and a lit cigarette in the other. Incense on long delicate sticks burned away on the ledge. There was a sober looking shrine on the small and squat reception desk near the doorway. The shrine held a picture of his own father, long and wild hair framing a sensitive and intelligent face. Intense eyes that seemed to always stare back, meeting the gaze of anyone who might stop for a moment to look. Fu Ren saw those eyes, the gentle slope of his father's nose, his sad impression of a smile.

Ren lifted the glass as he lay back, felt the cool burn slide down his throat, the ice cold and sharp against his upper lip. The radio rang on; he loved classical music, Eastern and Western, contemporary or classic in the truest sense. There was a universal sensuality, constrained and at once rambunctious and powerful, but always elegant and with intent. Timing and tune were essential. It was a lifelong delight of his.

He tilted his head back, bringing the brandy with it. The familiar sting mixed with the earthy acid of the smoke on his tongue, a nest of warm poison. The percussion rose, marching military against the flourishing brass. Fu Ren brought the brandy to bear again, his free hand tapping ash into a forest green ceramic tray he'd laid on the armrest. He felt the drink beginning to go to his head, a loving hand caressing something within his stomach.

Then came the noise of the door swung wide, hollow tin chimes tinkling as the frame struck them. Ren's heavy-lidded eyes slowly fought their way open as the slim form of his daughter entered the clinic.

"Good afternoon father. Working on the weekend?"

"Where have you been all morning, Lin?" Ren interrupted, sucking at his cigarette lightly.

"I had a few errands to run. Met up with a few friends at the noodle stand near the art studio," Lin offered.

"Oh yes? What did you order? Was it tasty?"

There was a brief pause as confusion clouded Lin's face; a few strands of her hair fell free as she shuffled foot to foot.

"Ummm... it was very good actually. We just had the bowl but we always ask for secret spice."

"I'll have to try that trick myself sometime," Ren replied, raising his glass above his shoulder rearward.

"Your mother is at home. She is not well today and couldn't make it in."

Concern knit Lin's already cross expression. Her normally playful voice took on a pique of concern.

"What do you mean not well? She was fine at dinner last night."

Dr. Ren dismissed his daughter with a

broad wave. "It doesn't matter, Lin. Go see her. Talk to her. I've had a long day."

Lin nodded and pressed her lips together. Whirling on her heel, the smoke curling about her shoulders, she exited the office, shutting the door behind her.

As Fu Ren continued to sip his brandy to the soft utterances of the radio, Lin moved along the dimly lit street towards the corner apartment the family called home. Fortunate to have an unattached dwelling, the Ren's nonetheless preferred to live near the office, for financial reasons as well as out of simple convenience. Cardboard boxes were strewn about the walkway – wet, flimsy, shifting beneath her shoes. She passed a speakeasy, soft conversation and muted laughter mingling with the musty scent of long-neglected ashtrays. Wrinkling her nose, Lin pushed on towards the corner of the avenue, now in sight, the simple painting of a lily marking the concrete next to the front door.

She entered, knocking politely on the wood as she did, so as to alert her mother.

"Mom? It's me. Where are you?" Lin called out, shrugging her coat off and tossing it on a nearby recliner. The living room was tidy as always; even in illness Mrs. Ren was an immaculate housekeeper. Lin figured she'd give her something to do, laughing a bit at the disheveled bundle of leather she'd just tossed over the chair. Ironically, she knew her mother would appreciate the small gesture.

"In here, Lin." Her mother's voice was hoarse, scratching out from the bedroom.

Lin poured herself a glass of water from the jug atop the counter, then turned and walked down the narrow hallway that branched off to their bedrooms. It was luxury enough to have her own room; Lin was alone amongst her friends in having a private space to call her own. She glanced into her bedroom as she passed by. Her records were still strewn across the bed, a small but sturdy oak bookshelf on the far wall was filled to bursting with books and trinkets she'd collected over the years inside the walled city, a few gathered from the bustling street ways on the fringes outside. All were untouched, in the precise positions she'd left them. Her mother's fastidious nature did not extend to the private domain of her daughter, an unspoken compact.

As she entered her parent's bedroom at the far end of the hall, Lin caught the strong scent of ginger, the tea resting on a small porcelain platter at her mother's lap. Wrinkled yet strong fingers cradled the cup, fingernails touching the gold-trimmed rim.

Lin met her mother's sparkling eyes, alight with playful fire despite the sickly condition of her voice, and a smile despite the pain. Inside every part of the sick woman's expression Lin saw a mother's undying love.

"Hello, Lin. So good to see you." Her mother sipped at the ginger tea delicately, having turned away from the window to look at her daughter. The midday sun entered in great force; they were one of the fortunate few to have an adjoining balcony and an unobstructed view of the street parallel. The commotion of business outside – hurried voices and running engines – blended with her mother's voice.

"Thank you, mother. How are you feeling?" Lin inquired.

"Better than yesterday, thank you. And you?"

"Very well. I just got back from seeing Dad at the office. He seems really worn out."

"Work will do that to you child," her mother replied with her sweet, cryptic smile.

"Do you think he'll be home for supper this evening? Did you want me to start something?"

"No, don't concern yourself with that, Lin. I'm not feeling very hungry and your father can cook his own supper. Go have fun. Your studies are very important, and I don't want you to catch whatever it is that I have."

"That's alright, Mom; I'll stay for a while and then head out."

So they sat for an hour, Lin looking out the window into the street below while her mother spoke to her softly, coughing at intervals, and finishing her tea. The sun felt so good on Lin's face; she leaned out, fingers grasping at the window frame as she overlooked her rusted balcony. Signs, neon and handwritten commingling, spread out as far as the eye could see in either direction. A cloud of pedestrians clogged the street below. Bicycles, motorcycles, and small cars hunched up against buses like herd beasts bundling up against a heavy rain. The smells of cooking meat and cigarette smoke were overlaid with exhaust fumes and, somewhere, the tiniest tease of salty ocean breeze from the bay. The thunderous approach of a jetliner skimming the top of the walled city drove Lin from the window at last, the deep vibrations from the jet engines thrumming through the wood and into her fingers.

After giving her mother a brief hug around frail shoulders, stooped with age and with the pain of her recent sickness, Lin made her exit, turning down the hallway into her room. Closing the door behind her, Lin moved to sit on the edge of the bed, moving her records aside and piling them up opposite her on top of the blankets. Standing again, she moved over to a tired looking turntable, the scratched and dusty glass covering the needle and arm as well as the surface of the latest rock n' roll import she'd managed to haggle at the second-floor market.

She lifted the glass covering the turntable and switched on the power, lifting the needle and dropping it in just the right place. Synthetic strings overlaid a deep and soulful bass signaling the earliest notes. She lowered the hinges on the glass while moving to the bookshelf beside the turntable, overfull, books and comics stacked messily on bowing chipboard shelves, black and glossy. Nothing stood out to her in particular amongst the well worn paperbacks, mostly fantasy and romance and the odd illustrated work. Little figurines, beautiful princesses and threatening warriors, graced what little space was left on the bowed shelves.

The song kicked into full gear over her shoulder, the vocalist barking out a staccato string of words violently. Lin found herself nodding along to the beat as her thin and intrepid fingers found the volume she'd been searching for, the split in the spine the sign.

A knock at the door interrupted her as she was pulling the book free.

"Come in?" It was almost a question; Lin was slightly startled.

It was her father; he didn't cross into her room, merely holding her eyes with a somewhat stern expression. Then he lifted her jacket from behind his back and arched an eyebrow.

"Yours, Lin? You know your mother isn't well. And the music, too loud."

"Yes, father," Lin sighed. He had never understood the relationship between mother and daughter. She took a few steps back to fiddle with the volume knob, dropping the bass.

"Better." Fu nodded curtly, still holding her jacket hooked over his fingers as if he were a piece of living furniture. He was smiling just the same, though, the craggy expression breaking as she approached him to snatch the jacket. She smelled the sweetness of the brandy on his breath.

"Did you spend some time with your mother? I hope she's well enough to return to work soon."

"We talked for an hour or so; she seems to be coming along just fine. As long as you have green tea in the house, she'll be on the mend."

Fu nodded again brusquely, turning away from the doorway in the direction of the bedroom he shared with his wife. As an afterthought, he heeled backwards and poked his head into view again.

"Oh, Lin. Don't forget your lessons this afternoon. You've been late too frequently."

This small lecture brought a scowl to Lin's face, wrinkling her forehead in a way that made her father smile despite the slight reproach. He disappeared around the corner and Lin could hear his voice warm immediately as he greeted his wife. Lin shut the door on them and turned the volume knob up again, though not nearly as loud as before.

She might have forgotten about her afternoon class had she not been reminded by both parents. Putting her hand to her lips and pacing about the room careful not to step on any loose vinyl underfoot, she started to think about where she'd placed all of her materials. A loose sheaf of paper sticking out beside the bookshelf reminded her – a piece of her sketchbook she'd torn free and placed there. The book itself was perched atop the shelf, the corner of the pad sticking out at an awkward angle. She stood on tiptoe and plucked it free. An open drawer revealed her brushes, charcoal, and coloured inks, some loose but most remaining in the box she carried back and forth to class. Gathering them all up, nodding her head to the hard-rock rhythm, Lin took a moment to survey herself in the mirror.

Her pastel sweater remained relatively unmussed despite the day's proceedings and having spent time earlier with Fang in that filthy box-bath. Her hair hung straight and loose across the cut of her shoulders. Her makeup, simple yet sophisticated, was also intact. She straightened herself and lifted the box, rattling, under the crook of her arm, along with her coat. Opening the door, she exited her room and turned toward the living room, hearing muffled laughter at her back as her parents shared a private joke. She tossed her jacket across the chair again, barely stifling more laughter, and once again exited to the street.

The walk to her lesson was not overly long, perhaps half an hour. Down the street lovingly known as Scurrying Mouse Lane and across a rickety footbridge spanning across another avenue, Lin did not linger. Only a few passersby greeted her on her journey – an old woman, straight and proud, barely leaning on her worn wooden cane as well as a gaggle of young girls shouting loudly and falling over one another. Scurrying Mouse Lane faded into Green Path, debris and graffiti intermingling with moss and mould, a miasma born of neglect and despair. Now she saw rows of beggars lying in their own sloth, though she was not foolish enough to stop to offer them her change. Like vultures, desperate and near death, a single shining coin would attract attention, and not the kind she was after.

Still, that didn't stop them from trying.

"Hey, miss. Money? Food?" a beaten and diseased looking old man croaked, leprous fingers extended. She stepped lightly out of his reach. More pleas followed, unheard as Lin hurried on.

And then they were behind her, again, left lonely in the darkened alleyway that marked the intersection between Green Path and the more populous White Market Lane. A reputable neighbourhood to be sure, by the standards of Kowloon Walled City, though the cracked and clogged veins that reached into the market were filled with trash of all sorts.

Lin merged into the flow of bodies, though there was ample room to move as mid-afternoon was not the busiest of times.

Entrepreneurs, legal and illegal, strolled the wide promenade, swagger in their step. Businessmen, appearing nearly indistinguishable in their fineries from her father and his associates dotted the crowd, their neatly trimmed moustaches, expensive spectacles, and new-looking topcoats marking them as a cut above the rest. The women, with their brightly coloured day dresses, paired very well with the dark-hued tones of their husbands and boyfriends, pointing out this and that item of interest with painted on smiles.

She stopped briefly beneath the awning of one of her favourite stalls, a jeweler whom had sold Fang a gorgeous brooch for their first anniversary a few months ago. A delicate and artistic rendition of a dragonfly, the brooch was bedecked with glistening stones in bright, eye-catching colours. Citrine and peridot swirls speckled the wings, wire-wrapped. Thinking back to the night that they had spent together – Fang's normally steady fingers pinning it to her chest in fumbling fashion – caused Lin's heart to quicken.

"Something wrong, young one?" The older lady tending the table shot over the wares, her forehead lined with years of worry. The scowl certainly didn't help her appear any more attractive.

"Oh no, no! Sorry. I was just thinking about how awkward my boyfriend was when he gave me one of your beautiful pieces," Lin smoothly covered. The bitter expression on the face of the shop-tender softened somewhat.

"Oh, I see. Which piece was it?"

"A dragonfly, covered in yellow and green gems."

"Ah, yes! I remember now. The fellow who bought it was a stranger to my eyes. I had never seen him before, and I'm very good with faces."

"Yes, Fang Shi. He's got a crooked nose and he's not very tall. I can see how you might remember him," Lin said.

"I have heard his name before. In whispers only. He was as quick with a smile as you are." Lin bowed slightly at the compliment.

"You've heard of him? How? I had no idea he was famous."

"For fighting, girl, fighting. Not something I know much about. His money was good and he was kind to me, is all I can speak to. Anything I can show you today?" The canny saleswoman detoured the conversation back to the matter at hand, and Lin declined, merely poring over the table while her conversation partner moved away to greet another potential customer.

An embroidered sapphire-blue cloth caught Lin's eye, artfully draped over the tabletop, folds like waves cresting over displays that had been placed beneath the fabric. A stunning necklace designed as a choker which could be lengthened for evening-wear was displayed prominently on top, pearls of grey, white, black, and pink knotted into the golden chain. She reached out to touch it, marveling at how smooth the freshwater pearls felt against her fingertips.

"How much for this one?" Lin cut in as the merchant and her customer, a dour looking man of advanced years himself, haggled. The older woman took a break in her conversation to toss the figure at Lin, who had to fight to keep her shock in check. Nearly two week's wages working at her father's clinic, no less. She slumped and nodded her understanding to the jeweler before moving along to her lesson, hoping the distraction hadn't made her late. She would make it to the yamen – her art studio – in time for her lesson, she reasoned after a quick mental calculation.

It was at the far end of White Market, tucked away in a corner bordering a physician's practice and an all-hours cafe, the aroma of tea and coffee wafting through the square and bringing with it an aire of comforting familiarity to Lin. She was almost there. As she approached the black and gold painted archway that led into the office of the artist in residence, Lin's mind shifted pace and settled on a more creative thrust, thinking of what she might want to work on today. Images flooded her mind almost immediately, a torrential thrust drowning her consciousness. She shook her head and walked under the archway, shifting the box beneath her arm into both hands.

The door to the studio was at the end of a long hallway, unlocked. As she entered, several students already deep in practice swiveled their heads to gaze at her, most of them returning to their work in an instant with a few lingering looks. They were mostly young men. As they too returned to the canvas, brush perches in their hands, she searched for an empty desk. Finding one at the far end of the rearmost row, next to a window, she made her way while snatching glances at the inspirations of her classmates. A rather shy little girl was working on a watercolour composed mainly from summer blues and greens, the flowers themselves artfully and delicately arranged despite her age. Two desks down, a wizened man with wispy hair was concocting an abstract work in shades of grey, each stroke pointing downwards with urgency. Her own desk beckoned to her, the chair pushed away against the wall, a slice of sunshine penetrating the cloudy window to cut across the surface. The walls were a faded yellow, trimmed with peeling wallpaper in a damasque pattern that looked to have been very expensive at one time, years ago.

She sat down and opened her artist's toolkit, charcoal spilling free, dusty and black. Lin pushed them to the side and shook the box slightly to dislodge her brushes and oil crayons. The pastels came out first, followed by a long brush with fraying ends and months of stain. She decided on pastels, collecting all of her various shades and lining them up neatly in the cubby beneath the tabletop. A shadow moved to blocked the sun as she felt someone approach; it was her instructor.

Tall, slender, with soft hands and soft features, her instructor was a man in his mid thirties. He was holding her canvas from last week, an unfinished piece. A hesitant smile was on his face, benign.

"Lin! I had not known if you were coming this week." His voice was even more delicate than his frame; he held the canvas out to her and moved out of the sunlight to stand beside her desk.

"Yes, Mr. Song. My mother is very sick and I was attending to her." That was partially true, and Lin was very good at lying so long as there was a kernel of fact.

"I am sorry to hear that Lin." His discomfort at this news was apparent in the lines that creased his forehead.

"Forget I said anything," Lin said, apologetically.

"Yes, well. I have your canvas here. You left it behind last time," Song said.

"I knew you'd take great care of it!" Lin smiled. He returned her warmth, the corners of his mouth tugging upward.

"Yes, well. It's very beautiful." He turned it about and placed it, along with a small, simple easel, on her desk.

The painting she was working on was something she'd seen in her mind's eye for some time now.

Before she slept, she would imagine the lines and curvature spinning around her, taking her away. The scene was of a stand of trees within a small meadow, the sun peeking out from behind a gossamer cloud. The sky was liquid cerulean, wrapped about the frame like spilled ink, without borders. She had drawn the harshest, hardest lines first in stark black paint, working her most delicate brush with confidence.

"Let me ask you something, Lin. If I may?" Song held his hands behind his back, swaying slightly.

She nodded, not taking her eyes away from her work.

"You've been coming now for almost a year, and each time you create something, it is bright. Outside. Is it because of your seat? Here, by the window?"

"I don't know, Mr. Song. I couldn't tell you where my dreams come from. I see these things when I close my eyes, and I want to see them with my eyes open. That's part of the reason I come here. You are the best instructor inside these walls."

"And what about outside these walls?" Self-aware levity entered Mr. Song's soft words, and though she couldn't see his expression, she knew he was attempting not to smile too broadly at her compliment.

"I wouldn't know; I so rarely leave. Errands and the odd time, I suppose."

"But you dream of it. It is something you desire," Song urged.

"Yes. Maybe someday I will see more of it for myself. I have never seen a meadow like this. A place beyond the sound of engines..."

As if to punctuate her philosophy, the

keening cry of another passenger jet descending to touch down at Kai Tak Airport pushed through the nearby window. Mr. Song lightly squeezed her shoulder before moving away, leaving her with one last thought.

"Someday may come sooner than you think, Lin. Change is coming to our lives," he said.

His parting comment brought to mind the talk surrounding the Ren family dinner table. Her father, his glass of brandy half-drained and his cheeks flushed, talking about all of the meetings he'd been attending with other professionals and business owners. Talk of relocation, resettlement – and, of course, the cash to go with it. The numbers seemed impossibly high for a government that had never reached out to them before, but with the British relinquishing the no-mans-land that was the walled city became something of a priority. She brushed all such thoughts aside, the obvious and nagging fear about Fang and their relationship was the last item on her mental list she crossed off before returning to her work.

For the next few hours, Lin sat in silence, the sounds and the sun receding to the back of her mind as she put her dreams to paper, her hands creating a portrait of her own future: a songbird on a branch, wings spread wide.

CHAPTER 4:

ROOFTOP ENCOUNTER

Bo treasured his time away from the watchful eye of Mr. Yeung, as well as his escape from the drudgery of endless lifting, pouring, mixing, and kneading that constituted his daily life. Most of all he treasured his escapes to the roof of the walled city, up the winding stairs and over the broken balconies to the very top. Though he was young, he'd not lost the desire for unsupervised play and pretend; the rooftops filled with rotting discards, furniture, and other assortments afforded this very thing.

Today, the sun was shining bright and hot on Bo's back as he crested the gutters and hauled himself upward onto the roof. A gaggle of gulls took flight with thumping wings as he did so, squawking at him in annoyance at having interrupted their latest meal of day-old scraps. He saw a half-eaten plate of noodles and vegetables that must have been the spoils, smirking at them, waving at the winged ones.

"Hey, come back! You didn't finish!" the boy called, laughing. The birds continued to circle, still shrieking their hatred at him as they sought a place to land, looking for new and better treasure to uncover. His attention wandered as the birds gave up. Their circles became longer and broader as they moved away from the huge structure that was the walled city, in search of other rooftops to pillage, bereft of irritating boys.

So Bo turned away from them and continued his quest for adventure amongst the rubble that was strewn atop the city like ruined ramparts of a long forgotten fortress. Sofas and recliners spilling sponge-foam from sodden wounds mingled with crushed beer cans and cigarette butts. Television and radio antennae stood out like wire frame gods and demons against the bright blue skyline and the great orb that was the sun.

The boy ran across the rooftop, his arms swinging wildly as he danced atop stained and discarded mattresses and leaves of losing lottery tickets. A few other groups of boys played at similar games, chasing one another with abandon, shrill voices pitched with anger and laughter alike. The odd couple, young and old, toured the uncertain edges of the building as if strolling along a seaside boardwalk. In a sense, it was. Between the slackened wires and broken furniture, the view of Kowloon Bay was spectacular today, only partially obscured by haze.

The walkways between buildings were dangerous at times, and Bo had the good sense and previous experience to know better than to cross at full steam. He slowed to a walk, chest heaving and legs dragging. The traverse was a simple matter, the wooden planks and steel supports screwed deep into both sides of the span. Nonetheless, Bo remembered many close calls when he and his friends had almost tumbled free and clear over the side to certain death. He could look to either side and see the pitted brickwork of the walls falling away into a pitch black abyss.

Finally reaching the other side of the narrow path, Bo leapt free and continued his run, making for a small and awkward structure at the other end of the roof he now sped across. At one corner ledge of the walled city, the asymmetrical shack was prime real estate despite being exposed to the elements; a dozen or more low-slung squatters' heaps were sprawled out in a broken circle surrounding it. Bo picked his way through these makeshift sleeping quarters made from old shopping bags, take-out boxes, wires, and burlap. The odour of piss and unwashed bodies assaulted his nostrils despite the open air and the general pollution; most of these piles of trash were currently inhabited. Bo could see bare feet sticking out from under a few of the heaps, the men inside either sleeping it off or napping away the afternoon heat.

Arranged to either side of the corner on which the structure sat were two glass and concrete shelters leading downwards into apartments. Barred windows wrapped in leaves and covered in condensation spoke to sunrooms where one might sit – even now Bo spotted an elderly man and what appeared to be his companion tending to their plants in their ersatz greenhouse. Bo took a better look as he approached his destination, squinting. Colourful lilies of all sorts wound their way up and around the bars, while some cooking herbs sat in squat pots, sprouting greens. The elderly couple worked slowly together, delicate hands working at the plants, adjusting them, moving one here and another there, maximizing the light of day. They held each other and their lips moved in pleasant conversation. It made Bo feel warmer inside than out; he missed his own grandparents. He'd never known his grandmother, and his grandfather had passed away when he was much younger. The only memories he had left were of a wizened yet expressive face, the smell of cloves, and an inexplicable happiness. He shook his head to remove the fog of his memories as he approached the metal shed.

The muscles in his legs tingled slightly with exertion, and he drew deep, full breaths. The rusted tin door in front of him swung open, and he was greeted by the gap-toothed grin of a familiar face.

"Bo! So good to see you," Liu said, tottering unsteadily out of the shack. He clutched a half-full bottle of dark liquor in his free hand.

"You, too, Liu," Bo said, moving forward to steady his friend, looping an arm about his waist.

"You here long?"

"For a while. To see you and the birds."

Liu cackled, throwing the bottle to his lips and drinking freely. Black liquid streamed from about the mouth of the bottle, dripping down his lips and jaw.

"Well, son, you're in for quite the treat today!"

With an expansive sweep of his arm, Liu gestured towards the shed. The door was already in the process of swinging open behind him and Bo peered beside the man to get a good look inside.

"Don't just stand there kid, come inside!" Liu attempted an awkward bow before turning his back on Bo and marching back into his building. Bo followed at a safe distance, ready to catch his friend should he fall backwards.

The shack smelled like shit as usual. Wire and cages of various size and condition were spread out all over the walls, even going so far as to partially occlude the single small window at the rear of the room. Chirps and warbles and other sounds reached Bo's ears, forming a strange animal symphony that somehow seemed to soothe him every time he visited. It was louder this time, more cacophonous, as many more pigeons occupied the cages than he remembered from last time. The strangest thing was their plumage, each bird dyed a bright shade from all colours of the rainbow. Bo's eyes widened as he took in the scene, his mind wandering from the feral scent of the room to the beautiful birds.

"Yeah, big race coming up, Bo. I dye them with colours so that the guys bettin' know which bird they're betting on. Easier to see the colours if it's night-time, too." Liu sat down on his rickety stool, sniffed, then brought the bottle up for another haul.

"They look so nice. It doesn't hurt them does it?"

"What, the colour? No, it's just dye. Besides, pigeons are good eating after they're done racing or carrying messages. Don't worry too much about them."

Bo bent over and gazed intently into the irregular rows of cages, walking slowly so he could get a look at each bird. Most were trim and slight, very different from the fatter pigeons he often saw perched on windowsills or on balcony ledges, strutting casually. To the boy they resembled prizefighters, proud and confident. Bo heard liquid sloshing around in the bottle behind him.

"You're almost old enough to bet, you know."

"I already do," Bo said.

"Mr. Yeung know about that?"

"He doesn't need to. It's my money; I earned it."

"True enough. There's lots of money in it if

you know how to pick a winner. Pigeons or pitfighting, it makes little difference."

"It's not about luck. Learned that from you, Liu."

The weathered face of the bird-keeper brightened at the praise. He leaned forward in his chair, gesturing conspiratorially to the boy with his bottle to come closer. As Bo leaned in, Liu whispered in a low tone.

"The only thing I ever taught you was that luck didn't exist. And, you know that well. What I'm going to tell you now is something you should also remember always. Fight and determination can only take a winner so far. The rest isn't fate, but what it is, I've never found out. Understand?"

This last said in response to the apparently confused expression Bo's face had adopted. Liu pushed ahead.

"And if you ever find yourself staring down a sure thing up against a whole lot of heart, make sure to put your money on the sure thing. Fate, like miracles, is a gambler's romance – complete with the heartbreak at the end."

"You sound like you know this personally."

"I do, kid. You learn more from experience than you do from any amount of planning or booklearning. It's the blows you get hit with that teach you about life, not the ones you avoid. Speaking of which..." Liu trailed off, hearing raised voices outside the shed and straining to hear.

"What's going on?" Bo asked.

"The fighter, son, the fighter. Shuto. The guy the Sun Ye On brought in to clean up in the ring. Destroy all comers, take all bets, and then put him on a boat to the next city. Called a ringer, kid. A sure thing. Heard he was gonna be here this afternoon for a demonstration."

"And you didn't tell me?" Bo slapped the older man on the arm in mock anger.

Liu smiled, his lips showing past the glass of the bottleneck. He let out a long belch before replying.

"Knew you'd show up to see how the birds were doing, especially since you're betting. And maybe to spend some time with an old drunk."

"A drunk who's still sharp enough to play the game," Bo said, smiling at Liu as the older man rose to his feet, knees cracking. Liu groaned as he gained his balance, placing a hand on his lower back.

"A drunk who doesn't necessarily like to drink." Liu's eyes were shut and he wobbled a bit unsteadily, finally leaning against a nearby bank of birdcages, his fingers wrapped about the wire like talons.

Bo moved forward to help but was waved away. Liu dropped the bottle with a ringing clatter and started shuffling forward, pushing Bo aside and then opening his door. The sound of excited voices and shouting could be heard. As they peered out of the doorway, Liu said one final thing, gesturing to the heaps of garbage and flesh dotting the concrete in a circle outside of his shack.

"Don't forget, Bo, these men are also gamblers. You are too smart to live like this. Don't start drinking. It's a hell of a path, and a path to hell. You'll start seeing things..."

Bo barely heard Liu's rambling, his attention fixed on a growing gathering of men on a nearby rooftop.

Most of them were wearing suits despite the hot afternoon sun beating down upon their shoulders. Black coats with white shirts, circling a man who looked distinctly out of place in nothing but a pair of nondescript grey shorts, his body heavily muscled.

Bo knew that these were the Sun Ye On, a gang that ran a minority interest in the city compared to the 14K, but nonetheless always sought new hooks to place inside her concrete veins. He'd seen the graffiti in more than one alleyway, the sign of the Sun Ye On rearing back like a hastily drawn death's head hanging over the prone body of many wastrels and beaten men. Such thoughts evaporated under the heat atop the buildings, the men in suits drawing further and further away from the man in the center.

"Shuto!" one called, a tall, thin man wearing a brightly coloured dinner shirt. The dark circles around his eyes and the grey in hair betrayed his advanced age. He raised his right arm, pointing towards the lone figure. If Shuto heard him, he made no sign of it, his bronzed flesh immobile, his eyes cast downward. He ordered his men to close in.

The gang members started to remove their jackets – all but one: the man in the dinner shirt. The rest, his lackeys, took deliberate care in their movements, never taking their eyes, hidden behind black sunglasses, from the man in their midst. They first removed their jackets, then dress shirts, white and black piles building up behind them as they cast aside their clothes. Though almost all of them were taller than the prize fighter, none of them were in his physical condition. Ink graced their flesh in contrast to Shuto's unmarked chest and back, rippling musculature over taut skin.

"We're going to see if he's worth the money now, boy," Liu whispered into his ear, the scent of rotgut liquor filling Bo's nostrils, causing him to wince and turn aside.

The shirtless soldiers of the Sun Ye On seemed hesitant to attack, slowly circling Shuto like lazy sharks, their eyes shooting back and forth between their intended prey and daring one another to approach first. Finally, one man worked up enough courage and rushed forward, a war-cry on his lips, fists raised.

Shuto moved forward to meet him, greeting the man with a lunge punch that struck full in the chest, throwing the gang member back, gagging, into a pile of garbage bags. Gasping for air, Shuto's victim raised his hands helplessly as another blow rained down upon his face, driving him downward into unconsciousness.

Shuto spun around to meet the men who rushed at him now as his back was turned, fear and anger written on each of their faces, tattoos covering their torsos. The largest of them pressed in, head bobbing and weaving, shoulders set for a grapple. As he cinched his arms about Shuto's waist and attempted to throw the stocky man, Shuto replied by driving fierce elbows downward into his skull with jackhammer intensity, driving him down into the dirt at his feet.

The remaining men halted just outside of the reach of the karateka. Shuto smiled at this, perfect teeth showing white behind his lips. Dropping his guard and stepping over the unconscious heap at his feet, he laughed breezily, a man clearly enjoying himself and his labours.

Two came at him from the flank. His leg snapped out and caught the leading gang-man in the stomach, driving the air from his belly in a great whoosh as he doubled over, then crumpled. The second closed with Shuto and aimed a knee at the mercenary's groin. Almost a blur, Shuto sidestepped the move and replied with a quick sweep of the leg, taking both out from under his assailant, sending the soldier of the Sun Ye On to the ground with a crippling crunch that signified broken bones.

The single man remaining shook his head in the negative as Shuto advanced on his position, his legs visibly shaking in terror. A black stain spread across the front of his trousers, showing even against the dark fabric of his dress pants. Shuto laughed aloud then, baritone booming, yet never taking his eyes away from the face of his enemy.

"Is this what you offer me, sons of the Sun Ye On? No wonder you have been hiding in this shitpile like whipped dogs!" Shuto bellowed. The sole standing gang member participating in the trial put his hands up in an attempt to supplicate Shuto, begging for mercy.

"Finish it, Shuto. Our money is what you're here to claim, not some sort of ancient pride that never was. So shut it and get to work." The brightly dressed man replied, voice as calm and even as a small forest spring, brooking no violence on the surface. Bo could now make out the grips of a pistol tucked into his waistband, and his eyes widened at the sight. Guns were a real rarity, even here in Kowloon. They spoke power as a threatening symbol and as a tool of indiscriminate death.

Shuto came within reach of the cowering Sun Ye On soldier and instantly snapped a hand out, grasping the man around the collarbone and pulling him inward, bringing his own skull forward to break across the bridge of the other man's nose. The snap of bone and cartilage told the tale; blood surged from the coward's ruined face as Shuto pushed him away like so much trash to slump over a nearby ventilation pipe. Shuto had barely even broken his stride. He was a giant of a man. He was a man who cast a long shadow.

"Seriously, Nianzu? Do you have any real prospects for me here or is this to be a parade? I have offers from Russia to America to fight for just as much money as you are offering me here, and in front of a real classy audience no less. Not in front of a bunch of drunken peasants that smell of piss and leftover meat." Shuto sneered, finally breaking eye contact with his employer to take a visual sweep of the battered bodies strewn about the rooftop. Those who weren't unconscious were groaning their despair, some cursing while attempting to tend their wounds.

Nianzu's lips tightened into a hard line. Bo crept to the edge of the building and leaned against the brick and mortar lining the edge, peering over, entranced by the scene.

"The money is all you should worry about. As for the quality of your opponents..." Nianzu waved a dismissive, veined hand, "that will be taken care of. You needn't be concerned about that. This was merely a test, to see if you were worth the great deal of effort it has taken to bring you here."

Shuto advanced on the gang boss, stopping a stone's toss away from him and squaring his shoulders, folding his arms so that his biceps stood out like great mountains. He closed his eyes for the first time and tilted his head back, jaw heavenward, allowing the warmth of the sun to soak into his skin.

"You know, if I close my eyes, I can nearly imagine that I'm not here, listening to you and your lies. I can believe that I am at home, in Okinawa, and that the breeze that blows against my cheek is tinged with salt rather than with shit. Your men are soft, as are your promises. You are right about one thing only, and that is that I'm here for the money and that I will be worth every bit of it."

"Looks like it. For now at least. Your first real fight is coming right up at the Siu Nin a Fu. The tournament. Remember the deal? Try to get some rest – if you need it. I'll see you down in the pit, tomorrow. First to fall... Ortega. Huge book in your favour, guy doesn't stand a chance. You won't even break a sweat. Capoiera, right? A joke. He's a dancer, not a warrior."

"Sounds good, *boss*," Shuto said, sarcastic emphasis on the last word. He hadn't moved since closing his eyes, still appearing to be in some form of trance, statuesque. "Now if you can get lost for a bit, I have some sun to catch."

Anger glinted in Nianzu's eyes, deflected by the sightless Shuto. Grinding his teeth, the mob boss stalked away, expensive heels clicking against the rubble of the rooftop. A few stones skittered crazily away underfoot as he retreated from the scene. Shuto remained still, immobile as the Sun Ye On men gathered themselves, helping one another stand, carrying each other away from the man who had wrecked them so easily.

Bo, Liu, and the great golden orb above stared at Shuto for many moments. A few of the drunks and drug addicts that had awoken from their filthy beds to watch the fight spat noisily before turning away from the railing and returning to their scraps. Clouds approached against the horizon, threatening rain. Eventually, and without a word, the statuesque figure of the karateka turned away from the sky and walked away, leaping from rooftop to rooftop when necessary, then disappeared down the staircase leading to one of the city's main arterials.

"Maybe it's time for your first drink after all, boy," Liu whispered, bloodshot eyes wide open.

Bo could do nothing but nod, offering his arm to help steady his older friend as they returned to the shack to talk of the birds, the bets, and the booze.

CHAPTER 5:

THE RARE PETAL

They held hands, drops of rain striking their faces and arms and running down to meet amidst their entangled fingers. Fang and Lin stood at the outer threshold of the city, facing west, looking out into a grey-black quagmire of a boulevard. The streets were near barren. Fang spied the scene of a young woman using a soaked newspaper as a makeshift umbrella passing by a drunkenly swerving rickshaw driver. The clatter of the rickshaw wheels against the uneven road set up a strange staccato with the heavy rain, almost overlaid, echoing against the banks of businesses that flanked the boulevard. As soon as the couple left the narrow alleyway carved into the side of Kowloon Walled City, they'd be drenched in seconds.

"Did you bring your umbrella?" Fang asked.

"Yes, just a moment," Lin replied, her fingers disappearing into the brown suede purse she kept slung over one shoulder. She'd worn some of her best clothes today, a navy blazer over a sunny yellow blouse and a tennis skirt that reached mid-thigh. Despite the rain, her hair remained straight, darker than night.

She found the handle of the umbrella and popped it open, sheltering them both. The raindrops drummed lightly against the thin canvas above their heads, punctuating their discussion as they pressed out into the street.

"You healed well. Back to your handsome self!" Lin smiled, turning her head to better appraise him.

"Thanks. Gentle touch goes a long way from a beautiful girl."

Lin turned away, blushing – but her grip tightened around his fingers.

"So where are we going, anyways?"

"You'll see. It's a surprise," Fang said smoothly. He led her down the sidewalk.

The street was wide enough to accommodate three or four lanes of traffic depending on the day, though it was now nearly deserted. A rust-coloured vehicle sped by, hi-beams shooting off into nothingness, rain obscuring both driver and any occupants. Another rickshaw, this one brightly painted in carnival colours, rattled by, carrying another young couple staring into each others eyes as if nothing else existed. The skyline was heavily obscured by a wall of signage that receded into the distance, each one painted a different colour. Each one bore bold fonts, some were illuminated with vibrant neon that glowed even through the light mist that accompanied the downpour. Grocers, tinkers, and scrap electronics shops dominated the urban landscape, a motley milieu that fit the neighbourhood nicely in Fang's imagination, joined by the odd restaurant or street-side bar that served whatever one could want to warm the inner hearth.

After a few minutes of pleasant conversation with Lin, Fang spied the sign he was looking for. Rare Petal Restaurant. He showed no sign of recognizing the place until they were beneath the hand-painted board proclaiming the entrance. Stopping suddenly, he pulled Lin tight against his chest, wrapping an arm about her waist.

"We're here. A surprise, for you." He kissed her, lips already wet. She laughed against him, pushing him back playfully and with a look of excitement.

"Here? Really? Isn't this place expensive?"

"What's expensive? You don't like it?" Fang teased.

"I love it. I mean, I'm sure I will. I've only heard about this restaurant from some of the clients at father's practice."

"Well, today, it's ours." Fang kissed her again, then stepped back and grandly gestured for her to lead the way.

Lin opened the door and stepped inside, Fang following closely. There was a small stairwell inside the door, immaculately kept stone steps leading upward to a simple mahogany door. Reaching the landing first, Fang held the door open for Lin, who thanked him and entered the restaurant proper.

She gasped, halting somewhat in her pace. The interior was splendorous, much larger on the inside than the small facade intimated. High ceilings were bedecked with golden chandeliers, each piece of crystal hanging heavily from a brass chain. Gorgeous floral murals spread from wall to wall, organically, emerald leaves mingling with sweeping petals, edges lined with expertise. The tables were few, modest in size yet rich in construction, aged wood covered with pure white linens. The tabletop was adorned with fine silver, glistening against candlelight cast from small wax globes artfully arranged. A single hostess was occupied with straightening and sweeping the tablecloths, looking up to greet her guests as soon as they'd entered.

"Welcome to the Rare Petal. For two?"

"Yes, madam. Reservations, actually. Fang Shi and Miss Ren."

Lin looked over to Fang, arching an eyebrow. This was not the usual noodle date. In fact, she'd never been on a date outside of the city walls.

"Ah. Certainly. Right this way, if you please." The hostess bowed curtly, head bobbing to one side, then briskly led the lovers to a table in the far corner of the small room, next to a window that overlooked the harbour. They sat down in the padded chairs, also carved from the same amber wood as the entrance. The hostess scurried away and returned in an instant, placing two paper menus the colour of ivory in front of the pair.

"I'll give you two a moment and be right back," the hostess said demurely before returning to her duties on the far side of the dining room.

The menu was simple, the script elegant

84

but not overdone, advertising a variety of delicacies. The wine list was brief but comprehensive, advertising several bottles of vintages crafted before either of them had been born. The prices were listed in simple numbers next to each offering, each one nearly ten times what the going rate would be for the usual walled city fare. Lin's furrowed brow gave Fang the impression – for the first time today – that she was anxious.

"Worried about the prices?" Fang guessed.

"Yes, Fang. I mean, we can't really afford this... can we?" Her timidity was showing, Fang had always found it highly attractive.

"We can. I'm treating you to what you deserve today. Order whatever you want."

"Are you sure?"

"Absolutely. I have a few extra coins from my last fight, and this is how I want to spend them. With you."

The hostess returned, a permanent and professional smile attached.

"Are the gentleman and lady ready to order?" she inquired, hands folded in front of her.

Fang looked questioningly at Lin; she nodded.

"I'll have the stir-fried beef, vegetables in

wine sauce. Carafe of house red also, please," Fang said.

"I'd like to have the seafood platter, please. I'll share his wine for now, and maybe more for dessert," Lin followed up, still slightly hesitant in her tone.

"Excellent. I'll speak to the chef immediately and be back with your wine," the hostess replied, making another stealthy exit, this time heading for the heavy swinging doors at the far end of the room, the racket of plates being stacked contained within. Moments later, she came back through the doors carrying a large decanter filled nearly to the brim with burgundy wine. Placing it beside the table unobtrusively, she was like a ghost, gone in an instant. This level of service was something Fang had never experienced, the hostess moving with the grace of a fighter and the delicacy of a martial artist. He was impressed, and it must have shown, for Lin called over the table for his attention.

"Not getting too interested in our waitress, I hope?" she said somewhat archly, though by the sparkle in her eyes it was clear she was teasing him rather than testing him.

"No, never, Lin. I just thought she was very impressive. No loud shouting or grouchy manners. No shambling or limping away to get a bowl of noodles off the line. Precise poise."

"I know what you mean, Fang. This is like something out of a dream," Lin sighed, picking up the carafe and lifting her wine glass to meet at the top. She poured herself a decent glass while turning to look out the window at the port below. The mild fog was starting to lift, showers abating. Now only a scattered, scant few drops pattered against the glass while the hundreds of huge container ships hauled their cargo about in the harbour. Great panels of metal dotted with rust clashed against the dark grey of the port water, engines thrumming deep below the surface while men, ant-like due to the distance, moved above decks, working machinery.

The food was finally served, brought out by the chef himself, a tall and distinguished figure. His face betrayed little emotion as he served each plate – the beef still sizzling and the seafood arrangement appearing fresh and colourful. The couple sat clutching the stems of their wineglasses in wonder at the richness of the meal, like something out of a long-dead fairytale. Their silence seemed to suit the chef just fine, bowing at the waist as he made his exit back towards the kitchen.

The beef was well-spiced and Fang ate

with gusto, piling noodles and meat together and dropping the combination into his mouth, relishing each bite. Lin was a more delicate diner, using her chopsticks to swirl shrimp in the heavy cream based sauce. Both of them said nothing, letting the enjoyment of the moment wash over them, the comfort of the food and the atmosphere enveloping them like the fog which had earlier threatened to dim the view of the harbour.

Then they poured more wine, and with it, sparkling conversation. They spoke of their fears – namely the fact that the relocation efforts seemed to be ramping up as the British finally released their grasp around the neck of Hong Kong. Where the walled city would fall was anyone's guess, though Fang was emphatic in his belief that his brothers would continue to run day to day operations and that nothing substantial would change due to a difference in political regimes. Lin wasn't so sure, some of the talk around ward councils and neighbourhood associations was that the police would be given orders to clean up the city, require permits and paperwork, and ensure the relocation of titled residents – people like her family, for example. Fang took another long sip from the goblet of red and refilled it from the carafe before replying, smoothing out the turmoil that resided inside on the matter.

"We'll be together, no matter what happens, Lin. I know that," he said.

"But, Fang... what if we move outside of the walls? They're offering my father a great deal to re-open his practice with all of the official credentials in another part of Kowloon. I heard my mother talking about it with him one night when they thought I was asleep," Lin replied, her brow a knot of trepidation.

"Shh..." Fang leaned over the table, creasing the perfect white of the embroidered linen. He brought his hand up to caress and cup her cheek. Lin smiled faintly despite herself.

Before they knew it, the red wine was gone, an empty carafe resting beside barren plates smeared with sauce. The date was done, and now the fog returned, thicker than before, and the rain resumed battering against the windowpane and cast itself into the water of the harbour. The waitress had come with her bill and it had been paid, in paper and coin, Fang rummaging through his pockets to come up with the sum plus a generous tip. Their tables were then swept clean, and they were ushered ever so politely out, the fixed smile of their hostess the last thing they saw as they descended the narrow staircase back to street level.

The umbrella snicked open again, heavy drumming as the rain snapped against it.

"Where to now?" Lin asked, hooking her arm about Fang's.

"How about a little bit of window shopping, and maybe a duck into an alleyway for a while?" Fang smiled archly. Lin squeezed his bicep excitedly and they were off, shoes clattering against the concrete sidewalk. The windows displaying various wares floated by as they walked, some advertising chintzy tourist items with bright paper tags while others, more muted and longstanding stores, preferred to show their finest goods. Rows of women's shoes caused them to pause, pumps, kitten heels, and flats all competing for Lin's attention. A pair of sunset orange ones with white lilies around the toe seemed to catch her eye the most.

"I'll buy them for you on the way back. Just a little bit further," Fang said, tugging gently at the crook of Lin's arm. Tan's Tailoring was just a half-block ahead, a diminutive and plain black and white sign poking out earnestly amongst the crowd, marking the corner that Fang was looking for. A narrow side street, never traveled but familiar to those who lived in the community, spread like a vein, bending back towards the harbour. After a bit of teasing and cajoling, the couple finally made it to Tan's, then turned down into the alleyway. A lone dumpster sat at the far end of the alleyway, dark grey paint flaking away to rust. A few broken crates and dented tin cans littered the cracked asphalt.

Lin pressed Fang up against the bricks immediately, her hands running over his chest. Her lips met his, she pressed against him, her arousal obvious. His own hands wrapped about her waist, drawing her closer to him, urgently kissing her, the umbrella forgotten and rivers of water washing down the brick around his back and shoulders.

"Well, doesn't that just break your heart?" A gravelly voice intoned sardonically. Lin gasped and jumped backwards, stumbling and splaying her arms out to catch herself against the opposite wall of the narrow passage. Fang, his mind still clouded and confused, fought to match the voice and face to a history, coming up empty. The man who had spoken was a tank, tall and broad-shouldered, muscular but having gone slightly to fat by the tautness of his dress-shirt, soaked through.

"Sure does, Lieutenant. Having to interrupt such sweetness. But she's too good a girl to be out with this trash." A second voice, this one high-pitched and nasal, belonging to a short, sparse man wearing a policeman's jacket. This man whined his threat while stepping out from behind the first speaker.

"You followed us?" Fang croaked, still reeling, trying to find his wits.

"Yeah, kid. Not that hard. You're a bit smaller than the average street tough around here, and there are only a few major exits out of the walled city. Plus, with a looker like that hanging off you, and the streets as empty as they are..." the big man let the message hang.

Fang ignored the rest of his bluster, turning to Lin. "Get out, that way. Don't let them catch you. Run!"

Fear registered as a flash in her eyes, but she was no wilting flower, immediately striding away from the men, her heels ringing out against the pavement in a regular rhythm.

"Well, now. That was stupid. We needed her for questioning. Would've folded and sold you down the river in a second. Radio the rest of the boys, Sergeant." The Lieutenant gestured towards his smaller partner without taking his eyes from Fang's,

"Meantime, we'll be taking you in." The officer began to advance down the alley with intent.

"For what? I haven't done anything wrong." Fang curled his fingers into his palms, forming a fist. The Lieutenant halted his advance, a look of amusement mingled with shock erasing the scowl on his broad face.

"For what, the little guy says. Hear that, Sergeant? Are you being serious, kid? We know you're with the 14K. We know you're one of the best fighters they've had in years. Do you think we don't have undercovers at the fights? You might be fast, kid, but not very smart."

"We'll see about that, asshole." Fang dropped into a fighting stance, hoping to buy Lin more time to escape. Running wasn't an option; he could hear more footsteps approaching from behind him in the alleyway, above the noise of the rain.

"You want to play rough? We've got back-up on the way, kid. Besides... I've got a few tricks of my own," the Lieutenant smirked, dropping his weight low and bull-rushing to meet Fang. Taken by surprise by the speed of the big man, Fang grunted in pain as the officer's shoulder took him just below the ribs, knocking the wind out of him. He felt himself lifted off his feet, then slammed painfully against a metal dumpster, pinned. A hollow, metallic echo mixed with his shout of surprise at having being taken so quickly. Fang felt a few weak punches against his stomach as the officer tried to find leverage while keeping him fixed against the pitted steel of the garbage container.

Fang dropped elbows down upon the back of the Lieutenant's thick neck, driving them deep into the flesh with a relentless fury. He heard the big man gasp, felt the grapple weaken, then brought up his knee in a vicious strike to the chest. The hold around his waist was released entirely, the large officer staggering back, clutching his chest. The Lieutenant's brow was furrowed, his eyes closed. He wobbled, then sat down heavily, his partner leaving his post at the end of the alleyway to rush to his side. The small Sergeant shot an accusing glare at Fang, reaching for his radio as he ran a hand over his superior's neck, checking his vitals.

"No time for that today, boss!" Fang called out, running away from the rapidly approaching footsteps behind him, leveling a vicious roundhouse at the crouched figure of the Sergeant, who had taken his eyes away from his suspect. Fang's leg moved through space in the blink of an eye, the momentum of his run aiding him as the full force of his foot struck the side of the Sergeant's skull, toppling him and the Lieutenant over into a messy pile of limbs and broken bones.

A gunshot rang out just as he exited the alleyway, powder from the brickwork spraying his cheek as Fang turned the corner.

"Stop! Halt! Get back here!" stern voices called out at his back. His legs kept pumping, his heart beating against his ribcage, adrenaline flowing through his veins, powering him forward.

What few passersby there had been moments earlier had evaporated, the street was now entirely empty. He could hear the urgent commands of the police backup more clearly now; they too had rounded the corner. Fang hoped that they couldn't keep him in their sights, or risk shooting a bystander in a nearby building – he crossed the street in a low crouch, zig-zagging as he scuttled behind a row of cars on the opposite side. Hearing another crack and the whine of a bullet ricocheting off the side of a nearby vehicle, his hopes sank while his heart thundered on.

He saw an opening leading down another slim side street just a few meters away from the rear of the car; he could hear the officers advancing on him, shooting randomly to keep him pinned down as they started to place him in a pincer. It was now or never. Fang rushed out from behind the car, running towards the alleyway. More gunshots rang out, again the sound of shattering glass as an abandoned storefront took the brunt of the damage in his wake. Coloured bunting and cheap secondhand clothes piled out between the jagged teeth of the broken window behind him. He could hear the nasal wail of police sirens approaching from far away. The alleyway here was much more crowded than the one he'd taken Lin into; garbage cans piled high and rats scurrying away from his heavy footfalls. An old, stained mattress and boxspring sagged lazily against the painted bricks. A bum wearing shabby clothes leaned near the far end, growing larger in Fang's vision as he ran closer. Fang swung his arm, cautioning the man to get down or get out, but received nothing but a dull gaze in return. Whether drugged, dumb, or simply defeated, the man didn't care to move. As Fang reached the other end of the alleyway and rounded the corner, a gun barked. Fang peered around the corner to see the downed figure of the homeless man, crimson splashed about his face and a neat black hole weeping from his temple.

Fang stood on a much smaller street now, this one looking much brighter and more populated than the last despite the downpour. Much noisier as well, which is why Fang supposed none of the tourists clogging the sidewalk had heard the violent end of the man in the alley. One of Hong Kong's many eccentricities, a thick river that ran from the bay into the heart of Kowloon, provided Fang with an escape plan. Dozens of small fishing and tourist taxi boats, low-slung, rocked against the cement sides of the waterway. Ignoring the stream of shoppers that threatened to push him along in the opposite direction, oblivious visitors to Kowloon district, Fang cut the line and scurried down to the nearest boat bearing a taxi sign. He clambered in, removing his coat and turning his back to the alley. The swarthy looking captain of the vessel, fully bearded, looked a bit askance at his new passenger. Strange things happened all the time in this part of the city, and so he wasn't too surprised when Fang spoke his destination.

"The walled city, fast as you can."

Over his passenger's shoulder, the boatsman saw a trio of what looked to be police officers emerge from an alleyway. He thought he could also spy a human hand on the pavement, lying limp near where they were standing.

"Don't look. Don't make a scene. They killed that man," Fang urged, hunching his shoulders while his eyes darted side to side anxiously. He looked supremely uncomfortable. The boatsman brought his eyes back to his rudder and oars. Grunting his assent, the muscular man set to it, setting the rudder and palming each oar, then straining as he pulled them through the water. The small ship began to move, the only sound now the laughter of the crowd and the metallic patter of a few last raindrops against the thin tin roof cast above the boat for shade.

After a few moments of tense silence, the boatsman checking every few minutes to see if the officers were following, Fang broke the silence.

"They are looking for us, aren't they?"

"Mmmhmm... Yes," The dark man rumbled from this throat, barely parting his lips to speak.

"Spotted us at all?" Fang asked. The boat rocked a bit as a large wave pushed up against the bow. Strange wooden chimes wrapped around one of the support posts for the makeshift roof jangled musically.

"No. They're headed the same way we are though. They'll probably beat us there."

"Just great... damn!" Fang cursed under his breath. They'd be crawling all over the entrances to the Walled City, his obvious destination. As soon as he tried anything, they'd have him in their grasp for sure.

"More than one way into the city. Don't have to tell you that," the boatsman offered, his face taking on a thoughtful cast as he pretended to stare out over the murky surface of the river.

"Yeah, and they'll have a badge and a gun on each and every one of those alleys. Not that they'd dare actually go inside themselves, but they don't need to," Fang replied, exasperation tinging his tone.

"Not talking about the ground," the boatsman said.

"The sewers? Not safe to breathe. Be dead before I ever made it. Puke my guts out on the way. That stuff only works in movies, friend."

"Not talking about the sewers." The look of cunning on the captain's face deepened, a twisted grin emerging across his sunburned features. He resembled a madman; Fang had clearly gotten lucky in his choice of carriage.

"What then? Sprout wings and fly...?" Fang

questioned, trailing off as realization dawned. The rooftops. Of course! There were several steel cables attached high above the streets. Some used them for clotheslines. Some maintained that they were for stability. Most cynics claimed that they were for hanging advertising and government banners – indeed, many of the steel braids were burdened with signs for shuttered speakeasies and long-dead campaigns. The once-bright script, now tattered and sun bleached, often torn and flapping like flags above the arterial, hid the long lengths of cable. The madman was right, a saviour in a small junk of a ship.

"You are beautiful." Fang smiled despite himself and the anxiety he felt inside.

"Excuse me?" The boatsman replied, startled for the first time.

"Said you were beautiful. Don't mean it like that. Just mean you may have saved my life today."

"Strange boy. Listen – you look like a good kid. And I don't much like police myself. Always harassing me about my papers and my registration. Shake me down a few times a year for more money than I make in a week. Makes me feel good to give back, you know?" The boatsman's face returned Fang's light, beatific. The two men sat in comfortable silence for the next moments, kindred spirits. A tune, a whistle, began to emerge from behind the beard, something simple and childish but happy – and for the remainder of the trip, Fang felt himself at ease. The foul weather persisted, coming hard again, wind pulling at the edges of the tin roof and causing it to clatter against the wet wood of the vessel's frame in strange syncopation.

Fang took the opportunity of the journey to take in his surroundings. He hadn't ridden the river leeching from the bay beyond since he was a small child. His family had been together, then, unbroken. He remembered his own laughter as his father lifted him up onto his shoulders, the boat swaying beneath them and threatening to slide and roll over. The turquoise water beneath them had sparkled at each knife-edge of the lapping waves, iridescent. He could hear the sharp jokes of his mother, scolding his father for his recklessness but secretly loving him for it. The idle, sunny ride from where the mouth of the bay met the city down to the terminus downtown, where the river narrowed to nothingness and they'd depart. There had been fried treats and sugary sweets then, his father and mother sitting together while he sat content with his snack food, the inner heat of the wooden table near the river's edge bleeding into his thighs and forearms as he ate. Most of that was gone, now, and what was left was deeply changed.

The bump of the boat's prow against the walls of the waterway signaled the end of their journey. The boatsman barely looked at Fang as he stood up, gaining his legs and preparing to exit the boat.

"I'm sorry I can't pay you much." Fang produced a few small coins from his pockets. The dark-skinned man frowned, waving the coins off.

"You need them a great deal more than I do, kid. You live in the city. My father lived there and told me a lot of stories about what happened inside of those walls. Don't worry about the coins. I never saw you."

"Thanks. For both favours." Fang nodded curtly, and stepped free of the small watercraft, stepping onto the small stone outcropping that served as a dock, then hurried up a flight of steps nearby to street level. The boatsman began whistling his strange tune again, fading as his oars took him away.

Of the few dozen buildings which were connected to the walled city by wire, Fang knew of at least two that were condemned, and had been for years. He had played inside of their crumbling confines as a child, the scent of old wood and dust stirring up old memories. Time was of the essence so he chose to head towards the closer of the pair, a ruined giant of a building that was nearly as tall as the top tier of his home.

Walking briskly, for running would attract the wrong sort of attention this close to the walled city, Fang strolled down the crowded sidewalk until he saw the abandoned tenement, kitty-corner to Kowloon Walled City, a multitude of clotheslines and advertising wires strung between the buildings. Some of them also looked to bear electrical wires, which Fang figured might be best to avoid.

He stepped into the shadow of the building, sticking close to the walls. A door off its hinges allowed him entry, swung wide, nearly leaning against the cracked masonry. He walked slowly, trying not to make much noise or to stumble over unseen objects as his eyes adjusted to the darkness within. He heard sounds of human activity, low voices – squatters – likely nothing to worry about.

As his vision returned to him, he saw the interior of the discount store that had once been here, dilapidated racks and pegboards in various states of decay about the large floor-level room. It was not quite as he remembered it. Many of the boards had been ripped apart and used for small fires, as could be seen by scorch marks littering the tiles beneath his feet blessed with small sacrifices of charcoal. A stairway at the far end, as best he could recall from his idle boyhood and the few times he'd visited before, led to the very top, level by level.

Ascending the stairs, the voices became louder. A murmured conversation started to become clear. One male, one female.

"Get any food when you went out?"

"No. All of the shops at the open-air market closed up as soon as it started pouring," a man's tenor spoke deliberately, calmly.

"Any ideas about what we can do to eat?" the woman said, a soft accent shaping her tone.

Dead silence rested for a few seconds.

"Nothing?" the male joked sourly.

Fang could see the two forms as he rounded the staircase and pressed up against the door frame. They were huddled together on the tile of the third floor, using a weak flashlight to illuminate themselves in the relative darkness. They were dressed in ragged clothing and looked like the worst of what the walled city could offer.

"Hey," Fang called out, softly. The two figures started, shoulders jerking in surprise.

"Who's that? Who's there?" the closer person replied, craning their neck about to stare at the intruder on the landing.

"A friend, if you want one." Fang stepped free of the landing, approaching the pair. They were sitting on a decrepit sofa, the arms falling off, legless. Their necks were craned over the back at an uncomfortable angle.

"Don't need any friends. Piss off," the woman's voice, though low and masculine, burred. She turned her withered face away from Fang. Her companion, a man sharing the middle-aged complexion of the woman, remained fixated on the newcomer.

"Fine. If you don't want to be friends, how about food? Got an idea about that," Fang offered. The woman once again turned around to meet his eyes. Dirt crisscrossed both of their faces. It was an invitation to continue.

"Look. I'll give you guys some money. Know a place just inside the city that sells some of the best noodles around. Yeung's. Not very far from that entrance." Fang lifted his arm to point in the general direction. "All you need to do is cause a scene while you're crossing the street. Big argument. Yelling at each other, stopping traffic."

"That's all? We argue every day. Part of the married territory," the husband piped up, drawing a biting look of white-lipped scorn from his wife seated next to him. Despite himself, Fang laughed, drawing the sharp look to himself.

"How much money?" The wife snapped in low tones. She didn't find the joke very funny, apparently.

"Enough." Fang produced a small wad of paper bills, fanning a few of them out. "Everything I have left."

Their eyes widened in the dim lighting of the wreckage, the flashlight swaying from the woman's grip, casting long shadows on the unfinished ceiling beams.

"I'll take that as a yes."

Still silence. Fang continued.

"You get half now and I'll meet you at Yeung's with the other half. Know better than to give you the whole deal at once."

The husband nodded his assent eagerly, while the wife looked even angrier, her scowl deepening. Fang wasn't sure if he could trust the likes of these, but he really had no other option and nothing to lose except a few bills.

The pair scurried up from the sofa and

snatched at the thin sheaf of paper in Fang's hand, neither of their eyes meeting his. Then they were gone, nothing but their retreating footsteps remaining to show evidence that they'd once lived in this bombed-out shell of a room. Fang turned away from the sight and returned to his ascent, climbing the stairs as his newfound friends sought the ground.

Moments later he found himself on the roof, scrambling over the pebbles and gravel to overlook the loose brickwork that fringed the top. The street below was sparsely populated, the rain having driven most of the traffic away. A few stray cars and rickshaws clambered down the lanes. A pair of suited men, clearly officers given their rigid carriage and look of authority, stood very near the entrance to the walled city, shades turning this way and that despite the lack of sunshine.

Metal cables, some spiked into the facade lining the roof and others clamped onto pipes jutting forth from the gravel and steel beneath his feet, sprawled out like cobwebs. Some hung slack, bowing earthward, while others seemed thick and taut, refusing to waver despite the slight breeze that played over Fang's face. The rain had intensified, though a sun shower seemed likely, light threatening to pierce the thick cloud cover hanging above.

Without wasting time, Fang chose a nearby tether and grasped it with both hands, choosing one bereft of clothing, bearing only a few motley looking pennants that flapped half-heartedly in the wind. The other end reached across the span of the street, seemingly secured to a thick exhaust pipe poking up above the rim of the walled city rooftop. Easing his body weight onto the cable to test its strength, he found it to have little give, holding up against the burden of his body as he began to crawl across, wrapping his legs about the braided cable and locking his ankles into place.

Fang was not afraid of heights, but kept his eyes entirely on the other end of the line, looking for instability in the anchor at his destination. Finding none, he shimmied across, feeling the slight sway as he reached the middle of the line. Hanging over the street, his ears straining to hear the raised voices of those below should they sight him, Fang pressed on, hand over hand. The rusted metal was rough beneath his palms, yet he could barely feel it as the blood rushed through his head, pounding. Rain beat against him, threatening to loosen his grip, dragging him downward in soaked clothing. He imagined himself falling, tumbling end over end, fingers curled skyward, then crashing like a broken puppet on the street below. He imagined horrified faces staring at him and then looking upward to stare at the ragged flags he'd clung to.

He felt the brittle plastic tear away as he rubbed against it – over halfway now – and in his mind's eye he saw the small wings of plastic flutter earthward.

The wind began to howl, ironically at the same time as Fang heard the argument he'd bought and paid for begin beneath him. Breaking his attention away from his destination, he turned his head to briefly survey the scene on the street.

"I told you, we don't have enough money to buy supper tonight!" a man yelled. Fang saw his plant trailing his wife, tugging at her soiled sleeve.

"Yeah, and I found you gambling last night at the Mah Jong parlour, losing everything I work for!" she shrieked. Fang saw the cops next to the narrow entryways pulling away from their posts nervously. Convincing actress, he thought to himself, pulling a smirk as he returned to the hand-over-hand.

"Work? You call that work?! I'm not exactly sure what the hell it is you do anyways? Always out on the town, dressed up!"

"Oh, so now the steady bum without a job

in years is going to tell me how to make my living? Our living?!" A true indignance crept into her voice and Fang's smile remained fixed in place. He was almost there. He could feel blood running from his hands over the wet cable now, knuckles white with the pressure. Pain was the last thing on his mind; adrenaline overruled it, flooding him, filling his spirit and urging him onward. He was almost there.

"Hey! What's this?" A new voice joined the couple. Fang chanced a glance at the newcomer and found it belonged to one of Hong Kong's finest, crouching down to inspect a blue scrap of plastic Fang had torn free during his passage.

Shit. Fang increased his pace, refusing to look down at the scene he imagined to be unfolding. Soon he found himself within arm's reach of the parapet, his fingers reaching out to touch the worn stone.

He heard another gunshot, echoing out from below. He felt the heat from he bullet pass by his cheek as he made the final few feet and wrapped his arms about the edge of the rooftop. Another gunshot rang out, he felt the chalky spray of powdered concrete against the skin of his face as the bullet ricocheted away, striking the masonry next to his nose.

He flung an arm and a leg over-top, then hauled the rest of himself over the rim. Two more sharp cracks barked out against the background noise of traffic and a few excited shrieks from curious onlookers. Fang could hear the alarm in their cries, many of them just seeing the last moments of his daredevil stunt.

"Fang?" a small voice called, somewhere to his side.

Fang rolled over, panting with exertion. Sweat ran down his neck, staining his collar. His head lolled and his vision was blurred, but he could make out a familiar form, a boy on the cusp of manhood.

"Fang?"

"Yeah." Fang coughed, clutching his ribs. He struggled to catch his breath, pressing on his chest. Dried and fresh blood both painting his shirt.

"I watch you fight," the voice belonged to a boy. Fang heard the awe in the slight voice.

"And? Go away kid. Having a hell of a day."

"Looks like you could use some help, Fang. Sure you want me to leave?"

Fang opened his eyes and turned to look at the young voice. The boy stared back at him evenly. The boy was holding a lit cigarette between his fingers, hand-rolled.

Like himself, the boy had a somewhat dark complexion complimented by a stoic yet severe expression. They might have been brothers if Fang didn't know better.

"Yeah. Yeah. Okay, kid. What's your name again? Definitely a familiar face. Can't quite place you though."

"Bo. I work for Mr. Yeung at the noodle shop."

Fang barked out a laugh at the coincidence.

"Yeah? I just sent a few customers your way. Couple arguing back on the street there. That's probably where I've seen you before."

Bo nodded, stepping forward to help Fang sit up against a nearby antenna array. Fang figured he could smell booze on the boy's breath.

"You need anything, Fang? You look pretty rough to me. Were those gunshots?"

"Yeah. Go to your boss and tell him I'll pay him for the meal those two are owed. If you see any of my friends on the way, tell them to find Lin and tell her I'm okay." Fang grunted as he struggled to stand, hands on knees.

Bo reluctantly backed away from Fang, looking as if he still wanted to linger. Fang waved him off as he finally managed to gain his footing, swaying slightly and leaning

112

against the long metal rods. Fang cursed viciously under his breath, trying to regain his strength. He looked up to find another familiar face approaching him at a brisk run.

It was Mei, a dark haired girl who hadn't yet been granted full access to the gang, an associate only. It was much harder for women to join, often-times assuming an auxiliary role – a blue lantern, they called her – someone who lights the way and scouts the path ahead. She was panting with exertion by the time she reached his side. They'd been an item in the recent past, before Lin's time.

"Fang! Everyone's out looking for you. I figured you'd be up here since..." she trailed off. He'd spent some time with Mei a few months before meeting Lin. It hadn't worked out for whatever reason that neither one of them could describe, though it had been fun while it lasted. The two of them had often escaped here to the rooftops, drinking beer and sharing tobacco.

"Yeah. It doesn't matter why you're here, Mei. I don't have time to talk. I need to find Lin."

"They've got her, Fang. Your brothers and sisters are out looking for you. The police outside asked a lot of questions."

"Who has her? The cops?"

113

"Yes. Apparently she was caught very soon after you took off. What happened? You look like hell."

Fang waved off her question, scowling.

"You want me to talk to the boss about this?" Mei asked.

"No. No. Tell Tai I'm coming to speak with him, nothing more. Tell him I'll deal with it."

"I hope so, Fang. This is big trouble. I mean they tried to kill you – shot at you! What if it's a trap?"

"It is a trap. A deadly one. And I'm going to set it off."

Mei shook her head, her eyes showing confusion and compassion all at once. Shrugging it off, she turned and ran away from Fang, towards the nearest set of stairs leading downwards to the Inside. She would tell the boss everything. She would tell the boss to expect Fang.

His brothers and sisters would pass judgment before he would ever be allowed to leave the Walled City again.

CHAPTER 6:

TAI, THE REDPOLE

The bar was bustling with activity, bristling with brothers of the 14K. Fang found himself sat nearly directly opposite to Tai, the walled city Redpole and thus the official spokesman for the brotherhood for all that took place within.

Empty beer bottles graced the pockmarked burgundy plastic of the tabletop, edges curling with age, condensation rings telling tales of gatherings long since lost to history. Neon lights advertising every vice flashed along the cement siding of the basement bar-room, side-by-side with glossy posters of the latest action stars. Rock music from overseas thumped out from the sound system stacked up in a corner adjacent to their table; Hane and a few of Fang's lower-ranking brothers fiddled with the receiver and argued about which cassette to put in next. There was a long bar carved from the finest cherrywood installed along the longest side of the subterranean den. Mei was standing behind it tending to the drink orders, wiping at the varnish with a clean linen rag between servings.

"Fang, we have a real fucking problem here!" Tai grimaced as he knocked back his fifth whiskey. The glass and the hand that cradled it came back down with deliberate heft.

"Yeah, boss. I know. Tell me about it." Fang didn't look away even though he would very much like to break eye contact. Weakness was not permitted amongst brothers and Fang had an image, and aspirations.

"Lin's still not back. The cops are still holding her. Mr. Ren is furious; he's already been trying to cut a deal with the cops for your head."

"And we can't touch him."

"Right. We can't. He's leaving anyways. You know he's going to take the resettlement offer. He just wants his daughter back and I can't really blame him," Tai sighed, tilting his glass idly.

"Me either," Fang said.

"No innocents, remember? We don't do

business that way. That's what you get for dating outside the circle, Fang. Told you that girl was no good for you. Told you."

"Yeah, but apparently I'm a little hard of hearing, Tai. You know listening has never been one of my strong suits," Fang joked, a fox's smile plastered on hard. Tai didn't return the favour.

"Fang, listen to me. This isn't a game. Two things need to happen here. You need to get the girl out of police custody – and I mean now. After that, you've got to beat Shuto. In that order. The brotherhood demands it of you. You took an oath to your family, and now our honour rests on your shoulders."

"Fuck, that's heavy," Fang said miserably, finally breaking eye contact with a weary nod.

"Yes... it is..." Tai said with a solemn air. A smile broke through and he clapped his old friend on the shoulder. "But you are just the man to do it. The boy from Yeung's Noodle Shop told me about your deception earlier today, and the climb over the cables spanning the street. Looks like all of that training comes in handy!" Tai's smile widened. He signaled for another shot with his left hand in the air while leaning back in his chair.

"Enough, Tai. I know what I have to do if I

want to honour our brothers and our fathers who came before us."

"Yes, I am sure that you do. Tonight, let's enjoy ourselves. Tomorrow, you begin in earnest. You fight for us all, brother!""

The meeting was adjourned as abruptly as it had began, Tai slamming down his shotglass after draining it again and pushing himself up on both hands. A group of newly initiated 14K fellows immediately swarmed him, seeing that the private audience had come to an end. Tai joined them in uproarious laughter and walked back towards the sound system. Fang smiled to himself, hiding his amusement behind folded hands. Tai had always been a fan of the old-style rock and roll music and after a few drinks was well-known to demand at least an hour of Elvis' greatest hits on repeat. Fang braced himself and then, too, pushed his chair away from the table, standing to seek the bar and Mei's company.

Her long hair shrouded her face as she leaned over the bar to grab a few beers for a thirsty Triad. He thanked her by tipping the neck of the beer at her, then stalked off, the back of his black leathers dotted with studs. He'd left a tip on the bartop, which Mei was just tucking into her pants pocket as Fang took a seat at the far end of the bar, closest to the cracked foundation wall. Fang saw her move to meet another potential customer as he stared at the rack of liquors behind the horseshoe shaped wooden bar. His attention wandered to the video gambling terminal in front of him, tumbling lights and sounds.

After a few minutes of fading concentration, his fingers idly picking at the label on his beer, Fang found himself looking up into Mei's eyes, sparkling with mischief.

"Hey, Fang. Hands feeling any better?" She smiled teasingly.

"Yeah, yeah. Thanks for asking." He raised his left hand up, palm outward. The gauze wraps around his hand were stained a deep rust-like brown – old blood.

"Bet the drinks help a bit, too. Want another?"

"Sure. Almost finished this one anyways." Fang proved the point by tipping back the bottle and downing the last dregs of the light lager. The taste was bitter in his mouth, but a practiced palate took little notice. Cheap beer all tasted the same.

"You look preoccupied. Usually you aren't this serious," Mei prodded, producing the beer and setting it down on a piece of cardboard in front of him, "... at least not when we're together."

Fang snatched the brew and immediately set to taking another sip. His brows came together in mild confusion.

"Haven't seen you in a while Mei, not since..."

"Not since Lin showed up. Yeah, yeah." The corners of Mei's immaculate smile dipped an almost imperceptible amount. "But that's not the reason."

"A goddamned lie!" Fang barked, laughing despite himself. Mei's eyes clouded over and her warmth vanished as quickly as her smile.

"Fang, you might be drunk, but you'll never call me a liar. I was over you and didn't want you to get hurt."

A lie in and of itself, and the knowledge of that rested between them both. After an uncomfortable beat, Fang cleared his throat and took another long pull, then used the back of his free hand, gauze and all, to wipe the wetness from his lips. He felt the courage booze afforded him building in his stomach, pressing his heart, urgent.

"Hear anything beyond what we talked about on the roof?" Fang changed the conversation.

"Not really. Just what you and all the other 14K guys are talking about. Deal is that you need to go see the police and get Lin out of there. Mr. Ren is an influential political figure within these walls and we don't need the additional pressure is the official line, I believe."

"Too smart for your own good, Mei. That's the shortest and most direct answer I've gotten all day, from anyone. Including Tai – but don't dare whisper that to him."

Fang nodded curtly towards the head of his family, who was currently swaying his hips to the rock rhythm of The King. Tai was a well-built man, nearly a match for Shuto, though not as muscular, favouring a leaner physique. Despite being a man of nearly five decades, Tai was still an imposing figure and spoke death as plainly as he spoke any other aspect of his personal truth. His sons loved him, and he loved them in equal measure. Such was the way of Fang's family.

"No such thing, Fang. Being smart is the only way to escape the worst parts of living in this hellhole. Unless you want to lay down and let the filth and the vermin wash over you like the passing of days, it takes a bit of a spark."

"A spark like we had? Or.." Fang trailed off. It was his time to tease back.

"A spark is something that trails off and dies as a cinder a moment later. We had something different than that, Fang. Not saying any more than that, or trying to muddle your thoughts any more than they already were. Just saying. It wasn't just a spark."

Fang nodded in silent agreement. The rock music grew in intensity, the speakers throwing forward all the thrust they could muster, cracked cones and all. Fang heard Tai cackle something about the new recruits, then the sound of breaking glass. Craning his neck about, Fang could see that Tai had thrown a full beer at the small slitted windows that were cut out near the ceiling of the subterranean barroom. He grinned at the display, watching as his leader exulted in the moment, shimmying with the best of the King's impersonators.

"Yeah," Fang replied to Mei without looking back, leaving their time together in the dust of days gone by. The night dragged on, the two making small talk over worn wood and little light, as their brothers and sisters drank themselves away.

CHAPTER 7:

THE LAW

AND THE BULL

There was pain.

Fluorescent lights stabbed deep through Fang's eyes into his skull. He raised bruised hands to shield his face from the flood of illumination, squinting. There was a plain metal table, burnished bright, in front of him. The walls themselves were painted black with burgundy trim, eating the light and imparting the impression of loneliness, surrounded by an expanse of nothingness. The plentiful rows of dull-grey filing cabinets and warped wooden desks spilling paperwork receded like mundane mountains guarding the valley of shadows and death. There was a threat here, silent before it was spoken to him.

"You take a dive or we take a dive on your girl, Fang. The hard way," a menacing voice crooned. Fang heard every word his interrogator said.

"Let me out of these cuffs and we'll see who hits the ground first, asshole," Fang rasped, returning his hands to the cool steel of the table. The handcuffs were wrapped about a thick steel bar bolted to the table; Fang wasn't going anywhere.

The officer opposite him, trollish, leered back. He was standing side-on, hands intertwined casually behind his back. The policeman's uniform was taut against his large, bullish frame. He carried a sidearm holstered at his hip, a cross-body band strapped about his bulging torso.

"Get paid too much to risk the pleasure of wiping you out right now, boy." The officer spoke while leaning forward and clearing his throat. Fang didn't wince; neither did the sick smile fade away from the ugly face of the man facing him.

"Looks like you've been sucking on the government tit for a long time," Fang said, raising his hand to point a finger at the developing gut on the officer, held in check with a braided leather belt.

This broke the big man's composure, he

wrenched his body about and slammed the table with two massive open palms. His eyes were as wide as a full moon, irises deep and disturbing craters.

"Look, you little piece of ghetto trash! I got a badge, you understand?! I am the law. But, badge or not, I'd break every goddamn bone in your body, you little –"

The door opened, shattering the moment. A smaller man closer in stature to Fang quietly clipped into the room, the latch whispering as the door shut behind him. His suit was neater than that of his counterpart that stood opposite Fang. His necktie was knotted perfectly and secured with a diamond tie-pin.

"Leave us, Bai," the small man said, voice smooth as silk. Still grinding his teeth, jaw muscles clenching visibly, big Bai complied and stalked away from the pair with heavy footfalls. The door slammed shut behind him. Fang and the small man were alone.

"Pretty courageous to taunt a man with a gun while you're chained," the man remarked idly, leaning back in his chair and reaching into the pocket of his blazer.

"Won't be tied up for long. Came here to answer a few questions, and still haven't been asked anything yet. Have a few questions of my own, as well."

"Such as?" the small man pulled a smoke free of his suit jacket along with a lighter.

"Your name, first off. Like to know who I'm talking to."

"I'm Captain Tong. I'm the one that sent Bai and his partner out to pick you up. Never told him to act like a buffoon about it. He has been formally reprimanded."

"... The guy who shot at me yesterday? Yeah, yeah. Now I recognize him. We all know that's what this is about. Big boy looks like just that kind of bitch to hold a grudge. Bad blood written all over his ugly face. Didn't like the way he got handled by me, earlier."

"Usually suspects aren't so forward in implicating themselves," Tong said calmly, lighting his cigarette and blowing a plume of smoke.

"All I said was the guy got what he deserved."

"That he did. And so will you if you don't drop the swagger. I don't like swagger. I like order."

"Well, seems we're at an impasse. I don't like order, and I don't like being jerked around like this without being told what the charges are."

"Assaulting a police officer is the first of many, along with multiple counts of drug dealing and gang violence. You're making quite the name for yourself, even outside the boundaries of the walled city, Mr. Shi."

"I like being a man with a reputation. Got any evidence beyond simple words?"

"Plenty."

Captain Tong reached into his breast pocket once again and pulled out a small orange envelope, tossing it on the table in front of Fang.

"Have a look for yourself," Tong said.

Fang reached forward and fumbled a bit with the small packet before finally managing to open it. The contents spilled out over the metal surface of the table. Lin was in half of the photographs, some of them taken while at his table on Heroin Strip. Yu was also in a few of them, seen handing over the little brown packets that earned their keep.

"How did you create these? Obvious forgeries." Fang kept his surprise from reaching his lips and his eyes. He kept his gaze fixed on the photographs for a moment longer before raising his face to meet the Captain's.

"Not so, and you're aware of that fact. Now, we move on to what we shall do with this evidence – particularly the evidence against Ms. Lin Ren, a co-conspirator of yours deeply involved in the drug trade herself. Perhaps she leverages her father's influence to peddle to wealthier clients?" Tong smirked, a look of smug satisfaction stealing across his face. It was a bad look for him, grotesque in execution.

"Leave her out of this, Tong," Fang said, threat in his voice. Tong laughed, the smoke bobbing between his lips.

"Or *what*, Mr. Shi? You're the one that's chained up in my precinct. With a stack of evidence against you and your collaborators. What possible leverage can you possibly bring to bear against me?"

Fang remained silent, rage building inside of his belly. He said nothing, staring arrows into Tong's skull. The Captain laughed again in genuine amusement.

"Actually, I've got a little surprise for you," Tong drawled, looking over to the door and gesturing at the small armorglass window with his free hand.

The heavy door swung wide again, and a hand pushed a woman inside, stumbling – Lin. Her face was bruised, purple and orange, a small trickle of blood running from her mouth. Both eyes were blackened, one nearly swollen shut.

"Lin!!!" Fang cried, attempting to stand up to rush to her side. The cuffs linked around the bar and wrenched his wrists painfully, jerking him back towards his seat. The table didn't move an inch despite the violence of his movement – bolted to the floor.

She heard him despite her confusion, turning her damaged face towards him, strands of jet-black hair falling to cover the worst of the abuse.

"Fang... Why? What have I done?" she said weakly.

Fang's reply was cut short by sharp laughter, Tong reveling in the moment. Fang's anger was wild; again he strained his wrists against the steel of the cuffs until they cut deep into the skin. Beads of blood began to form around the circular restraints.

"Lin! You did nothing wrong! These bastards hurt you, not me!!!"

She said nothing, still visibly shaking.

"Oh, come now Fang! You're the one that put her in danger. You're a criminal, a wanted man. You can't drag an innocent girl like this into your affairs," Tong crooned.

Fang remained standing, wrenching his wrists against the cuffs. His hands began to feel numb.

"That has nothing to do with her, Tong! Let her go, goddammit!!!"

Tong laughed again. "I don't think so, Mr. Shi. We have something else in mind."

Again, the door swung wide, and Bai returned to the room. He didn't take his eyes away from Fang, stalking him side-on, pacing in front of the table.

"I see the good lieutenant is still displeased with you, Fang. To be expected since you nearly put his brother in the hospital yesterday with those antics in the alleyway..." Tong trailed off as someone else followed Bai into the small interrogation chamber.

Shuto entered. His large physique and confident swagger was unmistakable. The fabric of his too-tight shirt swelled around his collarbone and biceps, his buttons straining as he folded his arms in front of him and leaned against the far wall with a cool nonchalance. He was barely visible, well outside of the light. Lin cringed as he swept into their company, shoulders lifting to cradle her neck. Shuto noticed and leered at her without breaking his composure.

"Oh, hello, sweetheart. I see you're still a bit nervous after our meeting earlier. I wonder – was I a little too rough with you?"

Fang's soul screamed. He could feel every muscle in his body straining to tear Shuto apart. His teeth pressed together, threatening to shatter, pain shooting through his nerves. Shuto saw his struggle and roared, his deep baritone flooding the room and causing Lin to shy away from him, edging into the darkness on the periphery of the room opposite him. Bai reached out and grasped her by the shoulders, meaty hands hooking into her flesh. Lin wriggled but Bai's strength was too great, he cinched her close and held her against his body. She stopped moving, eyes wet and wide with feral fear.

"I said *stay the hell away from her*!" Fang yelled, his eyes those of a madman.

"We will, we will," Tong said, "… as long as we can come to some form of agreement as to how the next forty-eight hours is going to go, that is. And that's entirely up to you, Fang Shi." Tong leaned back in the steel chair, blowing another spout of coiling ashen smoke. A slight haze began to build in the interminable night above, curling about the lampshade and dropping like a veil about them all.

Fang said nothing, too enraged to think clearly enough to respond.

"What we want, Fang, is for you to fight and win. Exactly what you've been doing and been aiming to do. There is a slight catch though…" Tong let the moment rest while Shuto and Bai looked on ominously, threats engraved on their thick jaws. "What we want is for you to fight until the semifinals, and then lose to Bai here."

"You mean you want me to take a dive? Against this piece of trash?" Fang spat, saliva flecking the table and landing near the ogrish officer's scuffed boots. Bai simply sneered in response, tightening his grip on Lin's shoulders with white knuckled force. She whimpered and crumpled into his arms.

"Shut the fuck up, kid," Bai growled.

"Gentlemen, please." Tong raised his arms and then lowered them indicating calm. There was an awkward beat before he continued, a hateful tension electric between the men. "Fang, you will do as you're told for two reasons. Calm yourself. Show yourself to be a man of the brotherhood rather than a wound-up drunk at the bar. Listen to me, and believe me – this is all in your best interest."

Fang flicked his eyes toward Tong.

"Very well then, I'll continue. You will lose to Bai after putting up a good fight. No obvious dives. This is about maintaining an illusion," Tong said.

"Like the illusion that I work for you? And fight against a dirty cop?"

"You do work for me. At least for a while. You'll put up a good fight and then hit the ground a few rounds in. Or submit, I don't give a shit which as long as you make it look damn good... real, you know? Convince the gamblers, that's all that matters... and the bookies – and the Sun Ye On." The edges of Tong's mouth ticked upward in a crooked grin.

"After all, Bai is involved in the drug game. Only difference is, Bai isn't 14K – he's Sun Ye On. Same as you, a high ranking soldier. Just like you, almost a Redpole. Unlike you, undercover. Not a true brother. But they don't suspect and never will. If you blow his cover – link me to the Sun Ye On? Lin dies. Remember that. He's safe for years to come. Bai beats you into the dirt, makes you his bitch..."

Tong's grin grew even more evil, malice eating through his mask of politeness. The plan was laid bare.

"Then Bai here goes on to square off against Shuto. And wins."

Fang gave Tong a distant stare, acknowledging nothing – in his own little world.

"... and of course, Bai takes down the ringer. Shuto is a sure thing against Bai – on the books. And you can guess where our department will be betting. Through an arm's length committee, of course. A gold chain that leads all the way back to my heart, you could say. But you never would, right Mr.

Shi?" Tong smiled then, and it looked sickly and unnatural on him, devilish even. The contrast thrown by the bright white light and the harsh edges of his bones caused Tong to resemble a demon, a graven statue, a gargoyle.

"You gonna let this fat loser take you out of the game, Shuto?" Fang said, still keeping his eye on the officer holding his lover.

"If the money's good, it's good. You wouldn't know much about that would you, little rat? Meaningless, fighting over scraps, beating up drunks and old men in a dying city." Shuto spoke with deliberate superiority.

Like magma overflowing from the furnace that is the heart of a volcano, Fang's rage spilled over, roiling into itself. Hate. Hate. Hate. The word repeated itself in his mind, branded his tongue, boiled his bones and set his skin aflame.

"I'm going to kill every last one of you sons of bitches," Fang rasped, crazed. He powered forward, cuffs snapping taut. The bolts clamping the steel desk to the earth squealed and whined, rattled. Yet Fang was held in place.

"No, kid. You're going to sleep. And so is your girl if you don't do what you're fucking told. To the very last word," Tong said, looking over to Shuto and nodding his assent.

Shuto moved forward and delivered a professional elbow, his hips twisting in perfect harmony with his torso, leading as if dancing. The blow struck Fang on the temple, just above his jaw, dead center. Delicate and delivered with beautiful brutality, the elbow pushed his thoughts from him into the blackened nothing.

CHAPTER 8:

RETURN

TO THE STRIP

Fang hurt all over. His hands hurt from the rough, frayed metal he'd swung hand over hand to his eventual escape. His wrists ached from the lacerations and bruising, having suffered scraping against the metal edges of the cuffs he'd been wearing up until a few hours ago. His head, his jaw, his nose – the pain was there. The drugs took most of the hurt away but not all.

An irregular island of stained cloth wound about his palms and wrists. Yu had teased him at first, up until he'd heard the whole story. Then Fang's oldest friend was pissed off, wanting to scour the whole city for the scum undercovers and the paid fighter that was going to take the ultimate dive for some dirty cops. The same cowardly cops that had for a full generation failed to brave the outermost gates of Kowloon Walled City. The same blackhearted bastards that had beaten and perhaps raped the woman he loved.

Thin snakes of steam floated and then dissipated before their eyes, hot pots of soup laid on the edges of their vendor's table on a particularly damp day. The warm rays of the sun did not reach here and so the hearty soup helped, sitting deep in the belly, curing some wounds that the chemicals could not. Fang and Yu recuperated together.

Fang chewed at a crispy piece of bacon from Viola's table. She'd looked at him with such concern that it had pained him, though he'd never admit it to his brothers. Men of the family didn't shed tears until honour was satisfied; that was the way of all things – their deepest and truest philosophy. It was as natural as breathing, as gaining one's footing, as putting one foot in front of the other. Tears did not stain the soul until all debts had been paid. Blood called for blood.

The sour yet spicy liquid splashed over his tongue and soothed his sore throat, bringing a bubbling cough to Fang's lips as he sat hunched on the stool behind the sagging wood that was his lot in life. It mingled with the salty crispness of the bacon, stinging his mouth. His lungs rattled after the beatdown he'd been delivered as part and parcel of the deal offered by the cops, Shuto in tow.

"The weight of the world on your shoulders, brother," Yu said thoughtfully, seated next to Fang on a similar stool, shoulders hunched forward.

"The weight of the world indeed, brother," Fang replied morosely. His bruises spoke for themselves, as did his body language. Shoulders sloped, slack spine, stomach splayed. Yu thought that Fang looked like a defeated man.

Two more regulars came then, plopping awkward elbows on the soft chipboard countertop and talking shit about the day's events, and those of last night. For the first time in many years, Fang had encountered a more interesting and potentially deadly evening than the average customer. The thought both terrified and amused him, breaking the peripheral halo of his fatal fixation for a few seconds at the least. The reprieve allowed him to recuperate, his machismo returning with a few frantic breaths in private. He expunged his doubt, spiritual fingers reaching down inside his guts and turning worms inside out, tossing them away in violent rejection. It was a gross process, leaving him comatose and dull for the majority of his shift, Yu taking the lead and dealing with customers like it was one of his better days.

Fang recalled his duties to his adoptive family. He remembered the sick rituals he'd endured to survive. The necks he'd slit. The corpses he'd buried, nameless and unmarked, beneath a layer of filth and sickly grey mud. The ones he hadn't even bothered to bury. As an agent of the most powerful family to have reached ascendance under the darkness eternal, Fang had lived as an antithesis to what ruled above, and without. In a land without law he was innocent; in a land of so-called civilized judgment he was eternally guilty. Each and every haunted husk of a man that approached the table, quivering with frailty, reminded him of the cost of his association. He was family to the reaper. He ruled on a throne of bone, made strong by siphoning the blood of his brothers. It was the spoils of a sick war, but one that raged eternally between those who thirsted for power and influence, particularly in an age of uneven sin and punishment.

"Looking deader than I am," an old crone cooed teasingly as she sauntered by, swaying in what little wind survived in the chamberous alley that was Heroin Strip. The street music played by the addicted minstrels about the hollow made it more natural, old joints locking into place to compliment the beat.

"Not anytime soon, grandmother," Fang replied quickly, bowing slightly to slip past the slight interaction. The elderly woman chuckled to herself; she moved away with a small smile. The moment was over. He had subjugated his fear, his anxiety, suppressed his soul, submitted it to the will of the warrior inside. The courage provided by his addictions reinforced his will. Fang felt normal again, whatever that meant to him. He was hooked up enough to take a hit whenever he so chose. He would need the hit to give him a hope in hell of competing tonight. Morals went out the window in a place like this, during times like these.

"You sure this shit don't bother you, man?" Yu asked. He turned side to side, the makeshift leather-scrap awning diverting water away from him, arcing down to splash amongst cracked concrete. By now, most of their customers had already taken their dose, clutching themselves tighter, snuggling into the lukewarm walls and tugging tight threadbare blankets.

Here in the dead of night, in a place where

no light lingered, not a soul slandered them. Bums, vagrants, the homeless – they existed here without reproach. Heroin Strip was where the unfortunate are born beyond pity, and then die. It wasn't the only home to these banal horrors. Heroin Strip was just the dead end of Lung Chun lane, pitch black, and not a glimmer of light dared to touch it. This was Fang's home. The same bleak void he claimed as his home was his source of strength; he did not fear the death of the light or the absence of hope.

That is fearlessness. No choice. Press on... Fang heard his warrior intone.

"No. Not sure. Certain. No other option. They've got my girl. Beat the piss out of her. Maybe raped her – I don't know. All I know is that I have a meeting with Tai and the brothers before the tournament tonight."

"Yeah? And what the fuck we gonna do about it? Can't let those cop bastards run roughshod over us. We own this fucking city! We built it!" Yu replied.

"Not anymore, Yu. Things are changing. We can stand against it, or like a dead fish, we can go along with the current. I'm for the former. And I hope Tai sees things the same way."

"He will, Fang. I know him. Besides, it's not like we can sit on the sidelines and let the

Sun Ye On call the shots in this city. That's a death warrant for everyone in here, us included."

Fang was fixated on the bright lanterns floating above, hanging motionless above Heroin Strip. He tried to keep his mind distracted, to keep it from running in weird and uncharted waters. More customers came and Yu tried to carry on the usual light conversation, laughing at times, sharing old jokes, treating long-time addicts like the lifelong friends they were. Yet they were still customers first, and Fang had no head for business today, his thoughts elsewhere, far away. The thought of letting Bai beat him down in the ring, dead center, for all to see – he could feel embarrassment and shame rising like a phoenix from the ashes of his pride. The lanterns weaved their small dance, barely moving, unless one imagined it. The neon splashes were the only stars they knew here, stars that were never exhausted, never extinguished. Thin, almost translucent paper separated the cavernous bazaar and those who suffered here from the light and the warms of the bulbs within.

"You need to go talk to your father, Fang. When was the last time you spoke?"

"About a month ago. He wasn't doing very well, and you know how it is. Men don't want company on the way out the door, you know?"

"No. You don't know that. All fathers care for their sons. Go see him." Yu said, reaching over from his perch on the rickety stool to lay his hand on his friend's shoulder.

"I will." Fang took the time to look Yu in the eye as he replied. He sighed and stood up, stretching and stifling a yawn.

"Now?" Yu said, confused. "I didn't mean right now, Fang. After work maybe?"

"Work can wait. I have shit to deal with today."

"Yeah, right. Right. I know. I'll hold down the business. You go deal with yours. Got your back, brother."

Fang nodded in return and walked out from behind the curved board and cinder blocks that constituted their table. He reached down and snatched up a few small brown packets while Yu was looking the other way. He'd never miss them.

The journey to his father's place was not a particularly long one, though it involved traversing a few sets of stairs. He clenched his fists, testing his grip, slowly unwinding the cloth from his palms as he shuffled upwards, one foot ahead of the other. They still hurt, though the food and the promise of another high helped him, moving his mental frame away from the shame he'd suffered and was yet to face.

His father lived near the rooftops, in the irregular storey just below the so-called ceiling of the city. The sun stretched through various portals here, touching those fortunate enough to have a facing window, or to live beneath a garbage grate. Many of the city's oldest residents took up a living here; fewer beggars and junkies were seen clinging to the concrete walls. Mineral stains streaked the low-slung ceilings.

The familiar aroma of roasted chicken reached Fang's nose, the intricate blend of herbs and spices used by the butcher's stall bringing back the fondest memories of Fang's youth. He passed the stall, waving at the owner who looked much the same as he had when Fang was but a boy, visiting his father before a dangerous mission. That had been quite some time ago. His father now enjoyed retirement from the family business that was the 14K, living outside of the active circle for many years. Cai Shi still drew a small pension from his sons and brothers, and he was afforded much respect within their ranks.

The narrow alleyway led over a stretch of scuffed boards and then metal grating covered over by cardboard, torn to shreds.

Scraps of paper, cigarette butts, and broken glass were swept to one side, forming a potpourri of debris. An electrical hum was also present, power lines stapled crudely into the stonework delivering stolen power along the length of the walkway, then down through drilled holes to the lower levels. Children rarely touched the wires twice, some completely live and uninsulated, and some children never survived the first test. Kowloon Walled City was deadly to those who did not know her ways, her idiosyncratic composition.

The walkway opened up eventually to a squarish plaza. Here, the walls were painted a deep forest green, brightening to emerald under the thrusting lances of sunlight that shot through the massive ventilating grate above. Discarded clothing, mostly rags, and other garbage settled atop the grate, blocking some of the illumination like a rotten cloak or a sickly shade tree. The golden glow that survived stretched downward to splay across the clay masonry of the 14K kwoon. Kung Fu and karate were taught there, both in equal measure, the fluid power of the former and the linear force of the latter combining in a lethal mixture. Fang's father lived around the wide promenade that extended about the perimeter of the kwoon, looking slightly down upon the structure. Fang leaned against the steel railing and gazed down at the kwoon, studying the form of the students, none of whom he recognized immediately, a sign of getting older, perhaps.

"Son," his father's voice called out to him, over his shoulder. Fang turned around.

His father sat as if behind jail bars, steel bars segmenting him from view. His home was very modest, a small booth with enough room for a half-sized mattress in one corner, a chair pushed up against a concrete countertop, and an end table opposite the open-air entrance. Crude shelves were screwed into the walls.

Fang walked through the doorway and reached for the fold-out camp chair that his father used to entertain guests, placing it against the wall adjacent to the end table so that he might look out the door while speaking to his father.

"Father. It is good to see you," Fang said politely, bowing in respect. He then snapped the chair open and set it down, the metal tubing scraping against the dirt and dust on the floor as he took his seat.

"Is it? It's been so long," his father replied wistfully, eyes squinting as he turned to look upon his son.

"I've been busy, father."

"So I've heard. Do you think that the news doesn't reach to the top of this city? That the old man who brought you into this world does not listen for whispers of what his son may be up to? You would be wrong on both counts," Fang's father rasped.

"What exactly have you heard? I'd be interested to know."

"Oho! Surprised now, are we? Well, Fang, I've heard a few mysteries. I've heard that you've become a name in the pit fights, the Siu Nin a Fu. This does not surprise me as you always had a talent for violence."

"Is this such a bad thing? After all, you were 14K before me," Fang said, uncertain of the direction this conversation was steering.

"It is not at all a bad thing. Not at all. The brotherhood thrives on violence. Death and the powerful threat of such has earned me a comfortable retirement, here, where I can see the sun rise and set. That and a flask of liquor and a pack of smokes each and every day, along with the gossip the boy brings me with it. I am an old man, and these are my comforts. They were earned in the same blood that now stains your hands. I do not regret it. Do you?"

A pregnant pause rested between them. Suddenly Fang was aware of the sweet smell of incense, the scent of cloves and sandalwood and camphor mingling together with a myriad of others. He shifted in his chair and saw a handful of lit sticks in front of his mother's framed photograph. Her smile was soft, tentative, hidden like a secret that only a select few would ever know. He forgot about that picture every time he visited.

"No. I don't regret it. It's how we survive within these walls. The brotherhood gave us everything we ever had. It would be dishonourable to turn our backs to the truth," Fang said, still looking at his mother's ghost.

"This is good. Good. And your hands? Torn to shreds? You can fight like this?" his father replied, eyes darting to Fang's bloodied and bruised fists.

"I can fight anytime, anywhere. The pain is far from me. I have discipline, and above all, anger," Fang smoldered, his own eyes narrowing, "...you taught me that, father."

"That may be true, but you'll need more than luck and wishes to win your woman back. Are the teachings of Cai Shi so revered that they defy common sense?" his father joked, laughter returning to his eyes. The smoke washed about them both, bring with it the sweetness of the past, when both of them had known the love of their lives.

"Your mother would not want you to fight without winning, you know," Cai finished on a more serious note.

"Mother wouldn't have approved at any rate," Fang replied, shaking his head, "she would have sought to protect me from the world as it is. No matter how far removed from reality."

"That is a mother's obligation. It is born out of love. A different love than the one we share, son, but as deep a love. Maybe deeper, for all of its naivete."

His father reached down to a caged locker screwed into the stone countertop, pulling a large bottle of liquor free. Amber in colour, golden, Fang knew it to be his father's favourite whiskey. Aged hands reached into the adjacent cage and produced two glass tumblers, opaque, milky with scratches. Though the hands that held the bottle were ancient, they were steady as stone, loose skin and varicose veins belying a weakness that didn't exist in the man sitting opposite Fang. A river of liquor streamed from the mouth of the bottle and half-filled the two tumblers. His father, grunting ever so slightly, twisted in his chair and leaned forward to offer his son a drink. Fang took it and cradled it between his thumb and forefinger thoughtfully.

"Mom wasn't naive or innocent. She knew the life we had to lead. She just chose to try and tint it her own way. She tried to make us better men than we were. Men of Yang instead of Yin. The bright lunar instead of the chaos ridden confusion. The darkness that haunts all men that live here." Fang took the whole shot at once, the fiery alcohol burning his lips and throat as it shot down into his belly.

"Fang, I knew your mother as a husband. As a lover. Besides you, she was my reason for living." Cai sighed, leaving it at that.

"And?"

"And without her, I still feel like a part of my soul is missing. That will never change. I learned this much years ago. But I still light the sticks, I still think of her. I still treasure her in my heart, as I know you do. What has come before helps us and guides us as to what will come. She is with us still, both of us." Fang's father finished his own glass in similar fashion, gulping down the amber. He beckoned for Fang to return his tumbler for a refill; Fang complied and the glasses were filled once more.

"So what do I do? They took Lin. They're holding her. If I lose, she goes free," Fang said.

"That's what they're telling you. Truth is,

it's the only card they hold. Lin. The woman you love. Do you love her? To the point of betraying your brothers? To the point of sacrificing them for her?"

Fang remained silent for a moment before speaking.

"I love her. She doesn't deserve any of this. This is something she never should have been involved with."

"Every woman who loves one of us, one of the men of the brotherhood, understands this Fang. She may have failed to understand the risks, but those risks exist. We take them gladly. Are those who choose to love and support us special in some way? Immune?" Cai said.

"Yes. She isn't equipped to handle this like I am."

"Are you? You're prepared to fail your brothers, empty their coffers on bets already made, bankrupt them in a time of uncertainty. Is this the loyalty that you swore to them? Over a pretty face and a bit of fun?"

"It's more than that, father!" Fang spat, lifting the glass to his lips and again draining the contents. The whiskey burned less this time, warm rather than volcanic.

"Is it? Youthful infatuation being one thing, family being another. How long has Yu stood by your side? How many times has Tai

151

covered your back in a bar-room brawl? How much of their own livelihoods rests on your fists and the damage they deal … inside the ring or outside of it?"

"And Lin's life? Is that nothing? Something to be tossed away like an old doll? A boring toy?"

"Lin comes from a wealthy family, big money. They roughed her up to get your attention, and the attention of her influential family. Influential, mind you, in a far different way than the brotherhood's sphere of power. It worked. They got your attention, and the attention of one of the most prominent legitimate businessmen within these walls. Now you need to call their bluff. You need to fight with everything you have. You need to win, Fang. They're going to do whatever they wish to Lin. Your performance tonight will make no difference. If you co-operate, she meets fate. If you struggle, she meets the same fate. They will either dispose of her or extort her family, as they have extorted you. The Sun Ye On have shown great dishonor by going to the authorities, selling their brotherhood to the police. They will not honour any agreement you have made with them. You must know this," Cai said to his son. The old man's drink shook in uncertain hands, excitement peering through the curtain of Cai's discipline.

"You didn't answer my question."

"I don't need to. You're your own man. I raised you to be a strong boy, a stronger man. Do you have what it takes to do what needs to be done without going weak in the knees?" Cai urged.

Fang said nothing for a few moments, taking in the small stall that his father spent his dwindling years inhabiting. A few empty booze bottles tumbled over one another behind his stool in a cobwebbed corner, newspaper covering their peeling labels. The spartan shelving, concrete screws and flat boards, bore the black and white photograph of his mother. The incense sticks bisected her picture from Fang's point of view, adding a somewhat macabre statement.

"I can't believe how much I miss her, after all these years," Cai lamented. He wheezed, coughing as he shifted to look at the same portrait that had hung on his wall for nearly a decade now. "It hurts me every day to know, as soon as I wake up, that it's another day where I'll never see her again, feel her hand on mine." His father's hand spasmed, as if it had shared in his reverie. He leaned forward, joints creaking and popping, cane cradled in his off-hand scraping the uneven, unfinished floor.

"Just know I did love you as I know you loved me. Next life, let's get it right, okay?"

Whether he was speaking to his son or his late wife, none present knew. Then the moment was gone, the dam broken, and the river of time flowed freely again. Fang's father had gone on a short journey to meet his deceased wife.

"I know how you feel, Fang. I'm not trying to be hard on you, or to tell you what you should do," his father said through a veil of tears.

"I know that, father," Fang said, fighting his own flood of emotion. He hadn't cried for as long as he could remember. Nor could he recall seeing his father show as much affection to his mother while she was still living. He could feel his mask breaking; he clasped both hands to the bridge of his nose and his lips to stop the tremors.

"But what you should do, and what a man must do... those words are sometimes islands, an ocean apart."

"That is the heart of the matter. What can I do? If I don't do what they say, they'll kill her. Or worse."

"You need to fight, Fang! And win! If they break you before you even enter the ring, you and your love are both dead. Make them

154

own the truth, make them prove they are the monsters they are – and your brothers will follow you into hell!" Cai stomped the butt of his cane against the ground, rattling the wood and lacquer of the staff and the dragon's head that rested atop it.

Fang bowed in reflection, folding his arms in front of his chest and letting his consciousness wander. He closed his eyes, listening to the world around him, the interior of a concrete coffin. No wind, no rustling of leaves, nothing but the hum of pirated electricity and the heavy breathing of his elder. Then, the sound of brass and drums. The kwoon was beginning a training session. The percussion reverberated, was absorbed, and returned from the strange angle surrounding the traditional temple. Fang and his father leaned forward on their stools, elbows on the stone shelf in front of the single barred window overlooking the scene.

The students wore their simple silk uniforms, all black with varying trim. This school favoured frugality and economy in all things, as was apparent by the depleted colour and condition of some of the garments. Nonetheless, though faded, none of the uniforms looked slovenly, even the most threadbare robe looking clean and recently washed, free of filth.

They paid homage to their instructor, their shifu. Then the forms began, their bodies in motion like individual works of art. Animalistic imitation blended with powerful strikes and perfect discipline as their movements were elicited by a whisper. Fang remembered his own time in formation, muscles moving in martial motion. He had learned to fight in the streets; he had honed his edge in the kwoon. Raw fury was the forge in which he thrust his barroom brawling skills, and he emerged from the tutelage of his shifu a new man, a hardened weapon of violence and vengeance.

Sunlit spears cast down upon the curved clay tiles that ran atop the kwoon in imperfect columns, tapering at the last to narrow gutters that swept away rainwater and garbage that filtered through the metal sieve above. The grate, rusted steel, spanned nearly the entire area of the room above. This was prime real estate, a place for retirees from the 14K and other successful businessmen to spend the last of their lives in relative peace and tranquility. The martial exercise and spiritual depth afforded by the view helped to offset the destitution of their small pensions. It was something to watch, a comfortable distraction, and a reminder of the virility and discipline of a youth that had earned them a place here.

The old wretches in the cavernous alleyways at ground level often had rusted, blood-crusty needles in their arms, pumping the cheap drugs that guys like Fang sold them. There was no morality attached to this; it simply was. Such nightmares were banished here, at least during the daytime, where the world outside peeked into the labyrinth and teased them all with a dream of what might have been, once. The promenade, fading into shadow at the edges of the grated portal above, was a route walked by dozens of those who lived and slept and woke in these tiny stalls. It was their patrol, their meeting place. Gossip was traded as freely as home-made wine and cigarettes and small, foil-wrapped sweets. From palm to wrinkled palm, history was passed down and along.

It was like a bleak postcard, something sold as a curiosity at the Kai Tak airport as Fang imagined it, though he had never set foot there, never crossed the threshold. The airport was a place of transience, of movement and escape, of people who appeared and disappeared never to return – should they wish. The opposite of his own city, Hak Nam, the city of eternal darkness. In many ways it was a prison, a place where one was born and one knew they would die, just like their parents and grandparents had. It wasn't all bad, brief bubbles of drink and drugs and camaraderie and commiseration drove a fierce sense of loyalty into their spines. The people he imagined walking by the flimsy display rack showing this photograph, this image, understood nothing of this, for their philosophy was shallow and far removed from the reality he and his fellow city dwellers experienced. For those smiling tourists and traveling businessmen, such a grotesque and asymmetrical snapshot of his actual life was an abstraction, an idle thought that one entertained for amusement rather than out of necessity.

Fang drained his drink, setting his empty tumbler down next to his father's elbow. The whiskey warmed his heart, emboldening him further. He smiled at his father and at the framed image of his mother beyond.

"Thanks. Gotta go. You helped."

Cai Shi merely nodded in reply, not quite knowing what to say. He sipped his drink and watched his son stand up and then brusquely walk away, through the open doorway and then down the promenade towards the tunnels that led far and away. He curled the staff in his free hand and tapped it thoughtfully against the hollow metal leg of his stool, beating out a basic rhythm that haunted his son as he stalked off into enclosed, eternal night.

An empty glass sat next to a half-empty one, both smelling of strong spirits. A small brown packet, unopened, waited nearby.

CHAPTER 9:

MYSTERIOUS

MISERY

Fu Ren and Mr. Song sat together, sharing a kettle of coffee in the dentist's office. Both men smoked slim cigarettes, puffing away in near silence, speaking only when necessary. Mr. Song had come to pay his respects to Mr. Ren and the two had ended up commiserating. The baby's breath in the blue vase now cradled a ruby-red rose, the lily having wilted away. The previously tidy shelving that rounded the room was now littered with empty glass bottles, liquor and beer. Some of the beer bottles were jammed with butts of extinguished smokes. Fu hadn't slept since the news that Lin had been taken, and all attempts to reach her lowlife lover had been fruitless, paid muscle blocking the way to the Heroin Strip.

Mr. Song broke the ice after nearly a half hour of awkward nothing where the two men sat and sipped at their cups, setting his drink down on the saucer with a clatter that backgrounded the murmuring of the radio. The daily news for Kowloon Walled City, Kowloon district, and the greater Hong Kong area was delivered in a barely animated baritone from the small speakers in the corner of the room, shiny aerial off at a jaunty angle.

"She will be returned to us, Mr. Ren. I have a deep feeling, here..." Song tapped himself over his left breast, his heart. Song had been secretly pouring some rum into his cup when he suspected the good dentist was not looking. His face hung, loose flesh, a crumpled body that betrayed his frailty and stooped shoulders that belied his aging frame. He sipped at his silver-rimmed teacup, both hands holding the small vessel. The rum in the tea was very strong.

"I believe, Mr. Song. I believe. And I know you care deeply for her. That is why I am glad you have come to me, tonight." Fu Ren spoke with an air of distraction, staring out into space. His mind and his thoughts were a world away and ages ago, rolling through old memories like film.

"The honour is mine, I believe. Lin always spoke – speaks – so fondly of you. Her favourite part of her day is spent with you, and under your instruction she has truly bloomed," Fu Ren said.

Song bowed his head. The room was darkened, only a handful of scented candles and the burning red-orange rings of incense sticks provided any frame of reference in the small professional practice. The scent of bleach and of various unnameable chemicals also permeated the place, smothered by the smoke but still present as a note, an afterthought. Song wondered if Mr. Ren could even smell the offensive chemicals anymore, trained so well by the hours spent working his trade here in the walled city without ventilation, indeed without oversight of any kind. Not that his customers, Mr. Song included, had ever complained about the work or the price. Song toyed with a large tooth at the back of his mouth, filled and capped, the molar having rotted away many years ago. Lin had been small then, scampering about the office, tugging at Song's pant leg and singing nonsense. She was always smiling, and that had, in turn, caused many others to return her constant cheer.

"Lin is a ray of light, something precious and rare, here, where we live. When she is gone we all feel it almost immediately. No one worse than her father... and mother," Song offered, his hand moving away from his cup to clap Fu Ren on the shoulder.

"Best not to speak of her," Fu Ren said, putting down his empty cup of coffee, placing hands on knees, and standing.

Mr. Ren wiped his hands idly on his neat khakis before shuffling past Song's chair, moving towards a small cabinet built into the wall next to the radio, fringes mottled with oxidization. The veneer had rubbed off in places, leaving bare but polished metal.

"Care for another drink, teacher Song?" the dentist said without looking back.

"Would love one. What's on offer?"

"Just plain rum, if you don't want tea with it."

"That'll do just fine. Been a day worthy of downing a few extra," Song said. The dentist grunted in agreement and swung to, holding the bottle in his fist.

"So, Mr. Song. Let us talk about Lin's work, something to take the mind off the current situation. What is she working on with you?"

"Lin likes to draw that which is beyond her reach. Beyond the walls. Outside. Everything she has ever done while working under me

163

has been in this vein. It is refreshing to see such talent paint beauty. I prefer it to the morbid and the grotesque which seems to fascinate so many of my other students."

"She has expressed this wish to me often – to leave, to live in a place where evil is the exception rather than the rule. I remind her, gently of course, that things outside are often no better than here, in the walled city. But you know the surety of youth, always certain that the light shines elsewhere and that they dwell in perpetual darkness."

"Some of which is brought on by the company one keeps," Song said, hinting obliquely.

"Ah, yes. You strike to the very heart of the matter. Fang Shi, that bastard. I can barely muster a smile when my daughter speaks of him. She says she loves him, as if she knows what love is!" Fu Ren was angry now, and sat down heavily, huffing.

"And so she says to me, also," Song replied smoothly, accepting the top-up of rum from Fu Ren.

"What the hell can she know about love – barely yet a woman?! I admit that there are few opportunities to date the sort of men that would be appropriate for her here, but she could surely do better than a drug dealing thug!"

Song knew better than to prod the angry animal inside of the man he was sitting and drinking with, letting the moment settle. After a few seconds, Song spoke his mind.

"Lin may know more than either of us, Mr. Ren. Remember what it was like to be young? Remember how sickening and smothering the attention of our own parents was? How binding and restrictive it felt, like every moment under their eye was like being in jail? Young women may feel this even more intensely than young men, for whom we at least give some allowance to be wild."

The movement of the dentist's mood reversed itself as suddenly as it had come on, he kicked the leg of his chair with the back of his heel and laughed at Mr. Song's philosophy.

"Too true, Song. Too true. So quickly we forget, eh?" Fu Ren remarked as he tossed back the whole shot of rum in one gulp, then quickly and adeptly poured himself a double.

The pair were interrupted, glass raised halfway, by a strong series of knocks at the door. Fu Ren dropped his glass, shattering on the tile and grout. The ruined glass was lying in liquid as he moved to stand. Song managed to keep his glass clutched to his chest, eyes widening at the intrusion.

"Expecting company?" Song stammered.

"No. Maybe it's Lin?!" Fu Ren gained his balance and strode towards the door.

Two steps before he could reach the threshold – his hand extended to take hold of the doorknob – the door burst open with explosive force. Fu Ren leapt back with surprising spryness, shrinking away from the open portal.

A hulking figure stood there, in the shadows beyond what little light the candles offered the room. He held something in his arms – something alive.

The shadowy figures swept into the room without warning.

CHAPTER 10:

BENEATH

A FALSE MOON

The noise from the room adjacent was distracting. Yelled wagers and the laughter of intoxication washed against the thick walls separating the brothers of the 14K from the great hall of the Siu Nin a Fu, or as Hane always liked to call it, the kumite. Two men stood on the platform, facing each other, and only one walked away. Any technique, any style, any path to victory was allowed. Tournament elimination was tonight's promise, eight of the best fighters within the Walled City had been summoned to compete for honour, glory, and cash. No press, no headlines, just word of mouth and reputation gained or lost in the eyes of the wasted souls who lived for the bloodsport. The lust for martial, sometimes mortal, combat was palpable, an electric effervescence that seeped through every pore of the men gathered here in Fang's dressing room.

Tai was here, as was Yu. Lifelong friends and brothers, Fang knew he could rely on them to his last breath. Even Mei was here, taking a night off from working the bar, her loyalty to the brotherhood – and to Fang – unwavering. She stood by the door, moving outside at intervals to ensure that nobody was eavesdropping. She flashed Fang a smile as she left the dressing room one final time, posting lookout.

There was an ironic solemnity to their meeting, the stormy moods contained within the mind of each brother contributing to its own energy, its own force. Long burgundy tapestries were evenly spaced about the room, hung from pipes above – some venting steam while others dripped condensation into small pools amidst the squat steel benches. A simple vanity carved by hand from some form of dark wood was nearby, propped against the wall as one leg seemed to be barely attached to the frame. Incense burned here too, cones, embers flitting from white hot through orange and down to an angry glow. The scent this time was filled with morbid memories, funerary, the smoke before a great battle. Pictures of famous fighters from the past, some in colour, some black and white, and some hand-drawn from recollection hung from spikes in the cement. All of them looked sober, serious to a fault, in service to something intangible and utterly primal. Death walked within the walled city this night.

"Fang, we love you. That is the first thing I want to say. I speak for all of us, here..." Tai said. All of the men looked at him; he looked at Fang. Some of the brothers broke away to share Tai's intense gaze, hands over hearts. "... and tonight, we will prove it. In living or in dying."

"I know my pleas will fall on deaf ears, my brothers, but I must ask it of you all anyway. Do not do this for me. My struggles are mine and mine alone. It is I who fell in love with the girl; it is I who must pay the price for such foolishness," Fang replied against a chorus of cheers from the fighting pit. None of the men looked to the door connecting the two rooms, rapt and focused on the undertaking at hand.

Tai shook his head from side to side, negating Fang's objections.

169

"No, brother Fang. Tonight is not about your failures, nor those of any man present. Tonight is about your trial. Tonight is about your ascension. Before the night is over you will be a hero, spoken of by all who live within our walls. You will bring great honour to our family. Before the night is over you will have your revenge, and you will have earned your place at my side, as a Redpole."

Eyebrows were raised and expressions of surprise showed themselves, but none spoke against Tai. Fang had already proven himself to be loyal to the 14K and all of the men here knew it. If they didn't, they wouldn't have come here. Some hadn't, preferring to skulk about the bar or find themselves too busy to lend a hand. Tai, Yu, and Fang knew the names of these men and would never forget their cowardice.

"Fang, my hand is yours." Tai bowed slightly, extending his fist, then snapping it back to his side.

"Fang, my hand is yours. Tonight's our night, man," Yu repeated both the verse and the motion, breaking the stone-cold atmosphere of the ceremony with a flippant grin. He flipped a butterfly knife out of nowhere and did a few flashy tricks with it. The other brothers laughed; even Tai cracked a smile.

Each of Fang's adoptive family took their turn at attention, delivering the oath. Tony Woo, the expatriate from America, his aviators reflecting a mirror image of Fang back at himself. Kwok, the older slumlord scrapper who had taken Fang on a few rough jobs shaking down tenants for back rent; he'd taught Fang a few dirty moves and the powerful truth that there was never such a thing as a "fair fight". Soon, the fresh-faced kid who just joined up about a year ago, full of piss and liquor and anything else he could get his hands on. His eyes were wild with excitement, adrenaline pumping him up to the highest high, an upward sloping arc without plateau. Many more souls stood with them, names Fang had seen in his waking days and deepest dreams since the day he was born. The family was with him, no matter how threatening the current circumstances.

Fear was present in all of them, buried deep and protected from view. Fang shared their fear, for it was his, radiating outward from each of them, tainting their chi, yet infusing it with imperative force. Fang flexed his muscles, stripped to the waist where he wore fitted shorts, black and gold. His lean frame responded, raring to go, tearing at his bones, urging his spirit on.

"You can do this, Fang," His father's voice

came from beyond the circle. They all turned to look at the old man, shuffling through the dressing room door, allowing the din beyond the door to pour in.

Fang simply nodded in reply, noticing the lunar shine in his father's eyes. The combination of hard liquor and hard drugs agreed with him; it was rare to see his father strong enough to leave his small cage upstairs. It was quite the trek to the fighting pits.

The small circle of brothers broke like a wave against an obstinate stone, allowing Fang's father to slowly join their ranks. Several of the younger men bowed their heads in honour of one of the eldest of their number, from the earliest days of what was written of their family. Some of the more mature men, Tai included, simply offered smiles to a friend they hadn't seen in a while.

Fang embraced his father, hugging him tight. His father pulled him into his own sunken chest, weaker than his son, fading with the passing of the days. Fang felt the old man's heart beat against his, in rhythm, reminding him of the blood bond that hummed in his ears and filled his muscles with the strength he still possessed.

"You can do this, my son." Mr. Shi grasped at his son's shoulders, craning his head back, staring at his son with far-off, starry eyes. He saw a warrior staring back at him. A warrior like he used to be. The crowd called for their warrior – their hero, or their victim, of the night.

"FANG SHI! FANG SHI! FANG SHI! FANG SHI!" the voices bombarded the room like an ancient battering ram, rattling the rickety door on its hinges.

"Listen to them. Tonight they will witness. They will speak of you long after I have gone from this world. They will sing praises of your feats of strength and dedication to the martial arts and to your family. You are our fists," Tai said, joining the father and the son. In many ways, both Tai and Mr. Shi had been responsible for raising the young delinquent after his mother had died. Then they thrust Fang forward – he stumbled – then caught the door handle and flung it wide.

"Get her back, okay?" Fang said thumping his chest with a closed fist. These were his last words before turning and beginning the walk through the damp concrete corridor that led to the tournament and the last word he would likely say to some of his brothers before they set off on their own fatal mission.

A few moments ticked away as each of the men strained to hear the shrill cries of the crowd as they saw Fang enter the arena, the dull roar exploding into something sublime, beyond explanation, deafening. The men felt the strength of their champion and his chi, binding them all and causing their souls to surge upward into their throats.

"All right. Everyone bring their blades? Pipes? Chains? Bad attitudes?" Tai said this last with a sneer, the joke cracking smiles around the circle. Kwok, Soon, and the others patted themselves down, most of them nodding, some of them pulling weapons from thin air, flourishing blades and bludgeons with practiced ease. Fang's father reached into the breast pocket of the suit jacket he'd been wearing for the last few months, then thrust his hand out. A few shining objects rolled about in the depths of his palm – bullets.

"Just my size," Tai said, taking the brass with care. He pulled a pistol free of his waistband and checked the magazine. "A few empty spots needed filling, after all." He fed the bullets into their berths, then snapped the magazine back into place and pulled the slide back. Mr. Shi nodded his approval before awkwardly staggering out the way he had came, the eyes of the brotherhood trailing him until he, too, was gone.

Tai nodded urgently at Yu, summoning

him close. Wrapping a friendly arm about Yu's shoulders, leaning in, Tai whispered to him.

"I need you to take Mei and to watch over Cai Shi. He's going to be in the crowd for sure, and we can't have anyone leaning on him. We're under enough pressure with Lin. Same thing with Mei; the Sun Ye On knows she meant something to Fang. Your job is to protect both."

Yu did not protest; he understood the gravity of the orders and agreed with the reasoning behind them. A slight wave of disappointment washed over his face at the news before he buried it beneath a stoic calm.

"Yes, Tai," Yu bowed to the Redpole, whirling on his heel to follow Fang's father. Tai heard a muffled conversation between Yu and Mei through the thin wood of the dressing room door, then their footfalls, retreating until they were gone. Tai turned to his men, bearing a savage countenance.

"Kill as many as you can. Time to drive the rats from our city," Tai said with a cold certitude. He clasped the gun with both hands and lead the gang out of the dressing room and into the shadows.

The streets were nearly empty this evening, most respectable citizens staying inside and bedding down for the night and most disreputable sorts arranged around the Siu Nin a Fu platforms for a night of drinking, smoking, whoring, and gambling against a backdrop of brutal violence. Tai and his family hoped to serve the same as the main course of the evening for their rivals, the Sun Ye On. Revenge was top of mind for them all, reclaiming their honour at the same time as lifting a cursed weight from the shoulders of their champion.

The clammy compartments filled with detritus and discarded clothing melded with human offal, getting worse as they proceeded through the maze of stairwells and shoddily-built scaffolds that was this part of Kowloon Walled City. Rusted plumbing, copper greening then eroding, dripped cold water onto their faces like tears as the pack ventured deeper. Flickering fluorescent signs, some intact, some busted up pretty badly, punctuated their journey onto Tai Yau street. It was dangerous enough to walk here during the day. During the night, anything could happen. Tai used to joke that they named it after him and the threat he represented to all who lived there.

They began to spread out as they entered Tai Yau. There was a small cafe on the corner, the tables and chairs left out even though there were no patrons at this hour. A few coffee cups that had been forgotten by the busboy graced the glass top of the table, the chairs themselves were at random angles, failing to have been pushed in – nothing worth stealing. Opposite the cafe, a laundromat remained open into the wee hours touching midnight. A handful of residents, most wearing weary faces, leaned against the ancient appliances while they waited for their laundry. The doors of the small business were pulled to and only the tinny beat of the washers and dryers tossing the clothes escaped.

Just outside of the circular light cast by the fading cage lights, ensconced in interrupted intervals alongside the thick stone pillars that flanked the street, a few figures approached. Leather jackets and tight denim pants seemed the uniform, with the striking symbol of the Sun Ye On patched onto the arms and chest pieces of many of the soldiers that emerged from the blackness beyond Tai's vision. Their numbers appeared about equal, although this patrol seemed leaderless – ill-equipped to deal with Tai and his men.

Both parties squared off in the middle of the impromptu intersection. The tight leather of the Sun Ye On and the bare arms and tattoos of the 14K closed ranks, leaving but an arm's length between them. The tension was thick. Those who had been wearing headphones removed them in anticipation of the brawl. Weapons were revealed on both sides. Tai's pistol was in full view. He waved it around when he said:

"Fuck off, boys. We're coming to take back what's ours. Respect."

At this, his gang snickered, throwing vulgar gestures out to the opposition. People were going to be hurt, and bad. There was a sense of menace that hung in the air.

"Listen, old men. Your time is over here. We have the girl. You understand? We play the game and take over this shithole. You bullshit boys walk away. You walk away now and you don't get hurt. Otherwise..." the leader of the Sun Ye On entourage, a short and sickly looking gangster with thick sunglasses draped over a long nose, let the ultimatum rest. That was a mistake.

"Here's your answer," Tai said, whipping the pistol in his hand up to the bridge of the short man's nose and pulling the trigger. The cool grin on the Sun Ye On lieutenant's face evaporated as the back of his skull exploded into vermilion streams and skull fragments. His corpse crumpled instantly in front of the

14K. Tai turned the gun on the thugs next to him and pulled the trigger twice each time, aiming for their center mass. He put down three of them before anyone reacted.

Then the men of the 14k lunged forward en masse, weapons glinting under the harsh, false, moonlight. The blade in Soon's hand was thirsty and snaked out, slashing at the face of a barrel-chested gangster. The blade struck true and carved a strip of flesh from the stout man's face, sending him away screaming. Kwok swung a thick length of chain at his chosen opponent, the heavy links striking the thigh and groin. The chain wrapped itself about the small Sun Ye On's leg and Kwok yanked it back with both hands, pulling the leg free and causing his opponent to crash heavily to the ground at a painfully awkward angle. The Sun Ye On enforcers seemed to be completely shaken by the savagery of their rivals and began to scatter, leaving their fallen brothers on the dirty floor. Blood seeped from weeping wounds.

Tai and his fellows checked their ranks, finding they hadn't taken a single casualty. Four of the opposing Triad gang members were cooling bodies on the floor. Two others were grievously injured and moaning piteously off to the side, one clutching his face where he would certainly be scarred for life, the other rocking back and forth, cradling a broken leg.

"You bastards want to live?" Tai rasped.

Both men nodded vigorously, though they did not stop their urgent ministrations of their injuries.

"That's good. You stay put. We see you move a muscle in our direction tonight and we'll end you."

The nodding continued, and Tai took a quick look around the alley to make sure the witnesses had cleared out during the skirmish. Most of the patrons of the all-night laundromat had scattered down the maze-like paths to their homes, wanting nothing to do with this. The rest were decidedly focused only on the spinning of their clothing and the dead hum of the machinery. No heroes here tonight.

Tai spun to face his soldiers, grim focus playing over his visage. In return, they gave him looks of feral bloodlust, galvanized by their victory, blood on fire. Tai pointed down the length of the lane, meandering away into visual oblivion. He led the way, shoulders square, and his family followed, mournful moans of ruined men in their wake.

CHAPTER 11:

THE SIU NIN A FU

The chamber that housed the great tournament was large, roughly square, with long benches and raised stands fanning out behind them for the cheaper seats. There was barely room for fight fans to stand, let alone sit. Tonight was the annual Siu Nin a Fu, the most brutal spectacle of violence money could pay for, beyond the law. Death was common, often encouraged when bad blood ran true between two warriors. Primal electricity sparked through the stone chamber, cries for each fighter ringing out and clashing against one another, torn from the throats of the men and women who'd won the right to attend this august festival of martial prowess, honour, and revenge. Nondescript walls during any other day of practice sparring and forms were now bearing great cloth standards embroidered with the names of champions past as well as the majestically adorned icons of the dragon, the tiger, and the demon.

Torches were lit along the periphery of the fighting platform at regular intervals. Thick wooden pillars, bearing a patina of wax and dust amidst intricate brass engravings, seemed to reach to the sky to arch and support the brickwork of the ceiling – a ceiling so cloaked in darkness that it seemed the night sky. The great height of the chamber demanded a certain gravitas, the torchlight reflecting off of the tops of the ornate columns, reaching fruitlessly in the attempt to pierce the veil of nothingness above.

Fang had emerged from the dressing room to a raucous rain of cheers. They had fallen on his head and shoulders as if an ancient gladiator entering the arena. There was little difference between the centuries then and now – though there would be no weapons in this show of shame and death. Hopeful souls fanned out from the edge of the platform like a tidal wave barely held at bay.

After his late entrance, there was a dearth of noise, just the murmuring brook of betting, the whispers of notes being rummaged through and passed between hands, and the elevated inebriation brought on by the drunks and the drug addicts.

The ceremony preceding the tournament began abruptly, a gong sounding and the crowd slowly wrangling their emotions into check, those able to do so taking their seats. After a few heartbeats, a trio of men wearing formal training attire in the various styles of Chinese martial arts walked out from behind the judging station placed in a crow's nest in the corner of the room, down a winding set of wooden stairs, through the mass of citizens, then onto the platform. The booth that housed them during the event was very basic. The same deeply stained wood that had been used to build the great support beams of the room had been used to build this structure in the high corner.

Each of the formally-dressed overseers stood facing outward, looking to the ticket-holders, an impartial look bordering boredom on their faces. Each of them was shorn of hair, bald heads shining with sweat in the flickering luminescence provided by the torchlight, enhancing the mystical ambiance of the evening. Then, one spoke, the officiant nearest to Fang. Fang was seated on one of two benches, four to each side, facing the other half of tonight's fighters, their knees nearly touching the taut canvas of the platform.

"Tonight, we are all gathered here to witness a life-changing event. The competition held here, in Kowloon Walled City, is the continuation of an ancient tradition by which we are all bound. Those who practice the martial arts are a different breed, men of pride and honour. Not soldiers, not thieves, but honour-bound warriors. Tonight the very best of these warriors from around the world will compete here, in the heart of the walled city, for the glory of being declared the very best. Their names will be written in history in blood, indelible."

With this, the first speaker fell silent, straightening his red and black kung-fu uniform. The second judge, a head taller than the first and with an uglier complexion, continued.

"This will be a contest between eight of the world's finest. All styles are welcome. Only one of the fighters tonight comes from within these walls, and only two from Hong Kong. The rest have flown across the ocean, traveled across the desert, traversed through the mountains and punishing plains to join us tonight in the martial spirit. All fights are to the finish, whereupon one contestant or

184

another quits or is unable to continue."

Some whoops from the audience threatened to spill over into an outbreak of cheering, but a glower from the tall judge towards the first offender, seated near the back benches, stifled the urge. The last man, shorter than the other two and wearing a robe of the Shaolin Order, took two steps forward to finish the opening officiating. His voice was stronger than the last two, a resonant bassy baritone that held all who heard him in thrall.

"There are rules, but very few. No eye gouging. No groin strikes. If accidental death occurs, such is the way of things – but no striking one's opponent when they have been rendered unconscious. Remember the spirit of the Dao, the code of those who pioneered these arts, and all will be well. Honour our ancestors! Tonight's victor shall join them in the halls of history!"

The Shaolin master spoke with such fierce strength and intensity as he ramped up his speech that the pillars themselves seemed to shake, dust falling free from the rafters to coat the head and shoulders of all assembled. A huge roar of acclimation and pent-up excitement burst forth from the emotional dam the judges had built, temporary and ramshackle. The crowd stood in unison and clapped one another in glee, madness in men's eyes as they waved their wagers and their beer bottles with wild abandon. Ignoring the mob, the three masters proceeded in the same solemn fashion as they had come, up the stairs, to once again sit in their chairs in the crow's nest overlooking the action, stone-faced and leaning over to speak softly to one another.

Fang was shocked to see Hane, his signature blonde hair bobbing and weaving as he sprinted up to the platform and reached for a dangling stage microphone that slid smoothly from the inky black above, a deus ex machina and a fine bit of stagecraft. Hane hadn't mentioned MC'ing tonight's event to Fang – which struck a sour note – yet he was happy to see his friend. Hane pranced about the platform, the stage being his and his alone for at least a little while, before he settled his circular weaving down a bit and brought the braided steel of the mic to his lips, posing dramatically.

"Ladies and gentlemen, are you ready for pain??? Are you ready for suffering??? Are you ready for revenge???" Hane's stage voice was stentorian and practiced, a lifetime of speaking over a thumping sound system had bred the art into him. Each of his successive questions brought even louder hoots, hollers, and whistles down from the seats. Hane's red leather jacket was draped over his shoulders nonchalantly, his fingers hooking the collar as he strutted the length of the squared fighting ring. He looked every part a gangster, from the smirk on his broad and shrewd face to the swagger in his stride.

"Then let it be done!!! Our first fight of the evening..." he drew this last out forever, allowing his own voice to meld with the hundreds in attendance. "Local favourite, Fang Shi!" – and now anarchy ensued – "... against the Russian Rocket, Yuri!"

Fang stood, slowly rotating his head from side to side to ease the tension in his neck and shoulders while adulation poured over him. It was simultaneously pleasant and yet intimidating in nature, urgent and demanding. His focus tuned them down to a dim echo in his mind while he focused on the face of his opponent, also gaining his feet from across the platform and doing a few shadow jabs to warm up a bit. Strong featured and severely maimed, Yuri had the look of a hardened Russian criminal. His stooped and careless posture ruled out a military background, and a cruel twist of the lip and dead eyes implied a killer instead. Fang moved his gaze across the opposing

187

bench. The Bull caught Fang looking at him, the knife-edged smile turned even more evil, the passion of punished flesh representing itself behind grey eyes. Fang looked away.

The crowd, like a Greek chorus, moved as one, leaning to see the two contestants as they stepped onto the cloth and wood platform. The fabric was a dull, dark blue to mute any stains. The boundaries were embroidered in a royal gold thread that lent an ironic majesty. At opposite corners, the two men stood stock still in anticipation of the call to begin. Hane had long since vacated the stage, relinquishing his microphone to the depths above, standing next to a nondescript and emotionless referee.

Then there was nothing but the space between them. Fang moved away from the perimeter and slowly circled Yuri, crouched low in a borrowed *kiba dachi* – horse-riding – stance, from shotokan. His own variation kept his fists at the fore, ready for a quick lunge. Fang could feel Shuto smile at him, piercing him at the nape of the neck, as he mirrored his move mentally, perfecting it, making it his own. Yuri had no such insight and simply waved off the stance as foolishness, spreading his outreached arms to the crowd as he circled Fang in turn. This continued until Yuri could bear it no more, his impatience driving him to clinch the circle, rushing forward with a battle cry that none in the room understood.

Fang shot a quick jab at Yuri as he closed ground, but the dodgy Russian slipped the punch and rolled his shoulder away, managing to grip Fang about the waist and cinch him in a hold. Wasting no time, Fang dropped his weight from kiba dachi, breaking Yuri's balance, then shot up, tumbling the big man backward, face twisted in the grotesque of abrupt surprise. Fluid, without breaking his forms, Fang moved into a kung-fu combination, quick hard strikes from his elbows and knuckles hammering down on Yuri's face before he could hit the ground. Fang flung a perfect elbow that caught the Russian wrestler in the jaw, and he felt the ligaments crack and give way. Yuri fell on his back and rolled over onto his knees, then powered to a standing position. Fang had not moved from his stance, rock solid, still, conserving his energy – waiting for the burly brawler to press him again.

Yuri grunted, both hands searching his face, his jaw, finding it hanging loose. Instead of fear or despair, rage flooded his eyes, his primitive features folding into a mask of war. Again he charged Fang, growling between slack lips, frothing like a madman.

This time, Fang was ready. He took a fast step forward as Yuri closed the gap, jumping in with a flying knee that caught the criminal directly between the eyes. Blood gushed from Yuri's nostrils. The big man fell heavily to the mat with finality. The spark in his eyes left him a crumpled form, his lower jaw hanging freely at an unnatural angle. It was over.

The audience erupted, exultant. Fang relaxed his stance, letting his muscles go lax, freeing his focus and returning to the world around him. He saw, outside of himself, his opponent lying prone, unmoving. He felt a masculine power grip him, reaching through his stomach to grasp his spinal column, shaking his spirit, thrilling him. Fang let the power wash over him, closing his eyes and tilting his head back. The white noise of the wall of sound washed over him. The fire, licking hungrily at the oiled rags and the old wood beneath, washed over his scars as well as his unmarked flesh. He felt free.

"Winner... FANG SHI!" Hane yelled, pumping his gloved fist in the air. Now the whole room shook, each person caught up in the emotional maelstrom. Fang was someone they all knew in one capacity or another – enemy, friend, family, or dealer. Fang bowed as he broke his casual pose. He took a brief look about those assembled. Shuto was doing anything but paying attention, almost ostentatious in his ignorance, his attention on a young woman sporting a low-cut blouse in the front row. The Bull nodded in a rare, ironic display of respect. False tattoos graced his craggy complexion, making him appear more exotic than usual, indistinguishable to those who might know him to see him passing on the street.

Fang jogged his way home to the bench, finding it still warm. While he took a seat, Fang saw Shuto break off the conversation with the heavy-breasted woman he'd been speaking with, folding his arms in relaxed fashion behind his neck. Shuto casually inclined his head, his eyes mere slits, smiling across the dark platform at Fang. Shuto spit, then resumed his great grin, awaiting his name to be listed amongst the hopefuls this night.

Hane cut through the chatter like a hot knife.

"Up next, in the second match of the evening! Coming all the way to entertain us from Salvador, Brazil! Formally trained for nearly two decades in the martial art of capoeira! Raul Ortega!"

A smattering of OR – TE – GA chants peppered those assembled, though the majority of the men simply booed the challenger, a plain looking man who immediately started performing cartwheels across the platform as soon as he'd hurdled the stairs. His pants were glittering – flashy silver on green, loose at the leg but tight at both waist and ankle. Raul moved as a blur, joints and muscles in motion, impressive despite his sallow chest and average physique. Bookies grinned at the slim 10:1 they'd placed on the exotic fighter when he finally presented, knowing that all of the no-hopers pushing their last cash on the exotic capoeira artist had just funded the weak odds on Shuto and then some.

Shuto simply hopped onto his corner without grandstanding. His name was announced by Hane with flair, a litany of victories that wowed the crowd. A delay was intolerable, action was in demand, and soon the metal against metal signal for the bout to begin filled the room.

The two squared off, both seeming very unimpressed with the other. Shuto immediately fell into *teiji-dachi*, a side stance, where Shuto faced Ortega obliquely.

Ortega warmed up in his corner, balancing himself on one limb and then another, showing grace and precision. Shuto moved to the middle of the ring, maintaining frame. Ortega came to meet him, light on his feet.

Ortega led with a flurry of dancing jabs, shifting his approach with each blow. Shuto, as if swatting a fly, touched each punch away with minimal effort, such that they breezed past his face. Ortega artfully flipped backwards and out of the range of Shuto's counterpunches, delivered in quick succession. Shuto's disappointment didn't reach beyond his inner dialogue to meet his face, and so Ortega found himself facing the unreadable.

Ortega flipped forward with alacrity, faster than most could see, guard up as he landed the jump.

Shuto cranked his hip about at the same time, predicting the approach. A vicious roundhouse reached out to hook hard into Ortega's midsection, under his guard. The sickening rip of ribs being shattered reverberated about the room, the sick detail silencing the crowd. A great gasp and a crooning of surprise complimented this physical theater, Ortega spewing bile and blood. His internal organs in mutiny, Ortega clawed at his breast with both hands, drawing white lines. His face was a rictus of agony, he dropped and curled against the canvas.

The referee rushed into the ring, throwing himself on the platform from the floor, reaching Ortega's side and turning him over. Ortega's lips were purple, flecked with the colour of coal. He coughed, hiccuped, and spasmed, spitting more crimson. Then he lie still. His skin lost its colour. There was a hollow wheeze and rattle, a weak cough racking his lungs.

"Dead. He's dead!!!" The referee shouted, waving his hands in a way that said he wanted nothing to do with this. Shuto stood nearby, staring down at the dead man dispassionately. Betting slips flew through the air, landing on unsuspecting shoulders. Drinks were shaken, angrily spilling their contents all over the shoes and the floorboard below. Some beers were thrown, shining aluminum catching the warmth of the torches and appearing as shooting stars. It was a drunkard's symphony of sympathy for the departed fighter, no matter how pathetic his performance had been. Shuto regarded him as a worm, diseased and unworthy, something he'd enjoyed as a diversion. There was no pause in the action as the referee and Hane worked together, each tugging a loose arm, dragging the body away into the darkness.

Passing the loose skeleton off to another handler, Hane promptly forgot about the man who was Ortega and once again focused on the show.

"Well, folks, we better goddamn believe that these two contests don't represent the rest of the night or else we'll be home before the goddamned kids are asleep. You hear me?!" Hane joked, ticketholders laughing and jostling each other. Trying to quiet down unsatisfied and unruly gamblers was just part of the job description for Hane, crowd control being his particular specialty.

Hane and Shuto observed the next two fights from the sidelines, a ring assistant busily massaging their muscles, pressing deep into the meat. Pain and pleasure melded and became one; relief merged with sick anticipation.

Yip, a Shaolin practitioner from a far-flung Chinese province, took the stage opposite Richards, a British kickboxer wearing pale blue shorts. While the kickboxer dominated the earlier rounds on technicality, scoring esoteric points, the Shaolin's few blows landed with such stunning accuracy as to sap the strength of his opponent. The taller, gangly kickboxer began to flag as time grew on, missing kicks with alarming frequency and allowing a studied counter-attack by the Shaolin at nearly every opportunity. Here a trip, there a throw – each time the crowd clapping modestly for the monk.

Richards, desperate, threw a ragged jump-kick at Yip's head, which the adept student aptly dodged, grasping the leg as it flew past and dragging the taller kickboxer to the ground. Richards' bruised body came down hard, striking a crossbeam beneath the platform full against the back, driving the wind from him. Yip, gaining position and a firm leverage about his knee with an arm bar supported by both legs, twisted as hard as he could. Yip's teeth came together as his arms did, a ferocious form. Richard's leg snapped like a brittle piece of straw, dry after a long summer. He shrieked, unmanned. The fight was over.

Hane sprang onto the stage with both feet planted almost as soon as Richards had given over. The mic dropped from above without grace, and he snatched it immediately.

"That's Yip! Shaolin Yip for everybody watching! House far outside the boundaries of Kowloon, and even Hong Kong. If he wins? We turn over all the prize money to renovate his kwoon and to feed the families of his village. The defeated? Sisko Richards, B-movie star and international kickboxing sensation! He wanted to win for his family..." Here, Hane paused a beat for comedic effect, spreading his arms wide to those hanging on his every word before snapping back into pose, pointing at the downed kickboxer.

"Hey, don't let the films jack you up too much Mr. Richards; you're still the real deal to me!" Hane taunted as Richards was rolled over onto a cloth stretcher between two poles, then carted away from memory. Now on to the next attraction.

"Eccentric Hong Kong business maven and part-time bodyguard for the Sun Ye On – the Bull, everybody! The animal who has a hundred trainers! Including the very best North American martial artists money can buy!" Bai stepped up on the stage wearing a tight-fitting track suit, then began peeling it off to laughing cheers.

A hulking form that dwarfed even the mountain that was the Bull calmly took his place opposite the undercover policeman, a great belly and soft facial features belying a certain interior power. At nearly seven feet fall and wearing the *mawashi*, the traditional garb of a sumo wrestler, it seemed a fit match indeed, with almost equal odds being bandied about by the pencil-lipped loan shark seated just behind Fang. The shrill, nasal cries of the gambler caused Fang's ears to ring; he briefly considered turning about and silencing the man before calming himself, tuning the noise out and focusing on the match – hoping the big sumo could stop Bai or at least slow him down a little.

"And in the other corner, a champion from many years past, though still in potential for reclaiming former glories! From the island I call my own home, and many here call something else..." Hane paused here, allowing for the cheap laugh to ripple through the stands, "... but at least twice, no three times my size. The real rikishi, the super-powered sumo – Jubei Otomo!" Hane finished the introductions with flair; the crowd was hot to close out the first elimination round and to move on to the semifinals.

The brassy resonance of the gong striking again set the two giants in motion, streaking towards one another in a straight line to the excitement of all, slamming into each other's clinch, a flesh thunderclap. Bai struggled to wrap his arms about the sumo, who shrugged off his attempt at a grapple, locking in his own, then quickly snapping his hips with unexpected agility to hurl the Bull to the floor. Bai came to a rolling stop, all elbows and knees, nearly off the edge of the platform. Without pause, Otomo merely strode towards Bai as the cop caught his footing, shaking his head.

Trying something different, Bai sidestepped the sumo – who was rushing in for another grab – delivering a few short rabbit-punches to the torso, trying to hurt the bigger man's ribs. A thick curtain of muscle and fat blocked his knuckles from driving home, the punches bouncing off harmlessly as Bai backpedaled away from a second set of grasping hands. The sumo was much faster than he looked.

Otomo looked slightly amused by the play, lifting his arms to inspect the damage to the jeering and crowing of the crowd. This time, the sumo stood in low-stance in the midst of the ring, lifting a thick-fingered hand to challenge the undercover cop to come take his prize. Bai obliged, barreling in low, hooking a leg around the back of Otomo's knee and shouldering into the sumo's solar plexus. Bai could feel the great lungs fold and shudder beneath the meat of his shoulder, the leg scooped free and the sumo's balance disrupted, hands flailing in the air until both men crashed to the canvas. Bai was still on top, pressing himself up and throwing punishing fists down onto Otomo's face, trying to break through his guard. One or two firm blows met home, snapping the sumo's head back, his short ponytail bouncing off the platform.

Sitting up out of nowhere with a reserve of strength, Otomo immediately encircled Bai's waist and then followed through with a huge elbow that caught Bai in the eye socket, blinding him and forcing him onto his own back, scrambling away awkwardly. Otomo took this opportunity to stand, then followed the prone Bull, trying to escape to the edge of the platform. Otomo was having nothing of it, stepping down with over three hundred pounds on Bai's leg, crushing it, pinning it underfoot. Bai cried out in pain, reflexively struggling with both hands, clawing at Otomo's ankle. In response, Otomo dropped a fierce knee across Bai's face, turning his neck around and knocking a tooth loose, the yellowed ivory spinning away in Bai's blurred vision. The audience boomed their approval, the sight of blood streaking the fabric driving them to frenzy.

The referee casually walked over to Bai, who was on his hands and knees, struggling to stand. The official took a sidelong glance, then walked back to his position beside Hane, who was chatting to him the whole time without response. Bai finally managed to stand, wobbly, when he once again felt two arms wrap about his chest, then pull him into an embrace. Both of his arms were stuck to his sides, and the iron band that was Otomo's tree-trunk arms continued to progressively squeeze the wind from him. He managed a few weak elbows which splashed harmlessly off the sumo's large stomach, a thin layer of fat rippling with each strike. The vice tightened, and now Bai could sense his energy – and his entire life – fading away.

With one final effort, driving both feet down as hard as he could, Bai sought to punish the sumo's instep. At least one heel struck true, from his uninjured leg; Bai could feel the splintering of small bones beneath his foot as he crushed Otomo's. The sumo let out a great bellow of pain and staggered back, falling onto his ass, feet splayed. Bai whirled about, his primal power pushed him forward, limping slightly as he hobbled to close the gap, leaping onto Otomo's chest with both knees, feeling the ribs give way. Otomo fell onto his back, raising his great arms in a weak guard. This time, Otomo was not able to defend himself from the flurry of straight punches and elbows that Bai buried into his skull, and before long, blood was gushing from the sumo's nose, ears, and eyes.

The gong sounded, barely audible above the whistling of the crowd. Bai felt a pair of smaller, softer hands reach up under his armpits, pulling him away gently but forcefully. He whirled, face twisted, fists raised to take on this new attacker. It was the referee, fear written upon him. Bai lowered his fists, letting the throbbing subside in his head, trying to slow his heart and the great heave of his breath. Drops of crimson-black fell from his knuckles, thin streams of the same ran from his elbows to encircle his wrists and palms.

Bai shot Fang a weary, gap-toothed grin, not even pausing so long as to have the referee lift his arm in victory. Hane scuttled onstage, smoothing his suit before announcing the end of the preliminaries.

"What a contest! What a spectacle! The Bull tramples the traditionalist, but only by a stroke of fortune – or was it something more? This mystery and many others shall be resolved, as we enter the semifinals!" Hane spoke with melodrama into the microphone. A few scattered pieces of hollering and applause punctuated his short remarks.

The audience began to disperse, yet cluster, many turning their backs on the stage to consult with friends and drinking buddies on which way to lay some money down on the games to come.

During the intermission, some of the fighters rose to stretch aching or tense muscles, shadowboxing or practicing holds. Fang simply sat, hands on knees, scanning the crowd for familiar faces to take the edge off. Some flicker of recognition caught him as he spotted a boy far too young to be attending tonight's festivities buried in the wall of faces and limbs opposite. It was Bo, the kid from the noodle shop, the kid that had helped him on the rooftop. He was standing next to the drunkard whose name Fang couldn't quite recall, but he'd often seen with the boy. He waved at Bo, smiling. The boy returned with a lopsided smirk, puffing his chest out and putting up his fists. Fang laughed, wiping beads of sweat from his brow.

"Something funny, asshole?" Fang turned to find Bai staring him down, arms folded, looking a little worse for the wear from his fight with Otomo. The hole in his mouth was obvious and distracting. He had actually lost more than one tooth at the hands of the big sumo, Fang noted.

"Yeah, how fucked up your face is. Hope you have better insurance than the average cop," Fang said. His voice was low and murderous.

Bai threw his head back in mad laughter, then brought a viper's eye to meet Fang's. "Kid, you have no idea what I'm going to do with you when it's just us in the ring. I have all the time in the world, remember? Your lady friend is ours. And if you don't let me work you over, as long as I fucking well want, she's dead."

Fang said nothing in reply, grinding his jaw.

"Yeah, that's what I thought you little piece of trash! You're a nobody. A never was. And I'm going to hurt you real bad tonight. Real bad. And after that, it's your pretty little piece's turn! Believe that." Bai curled his lip and spat on the floor at Fang's back before sauntering back to his position on the opposing bench.

Fang turned back to Bo, seeing that the kid had observed the entire encounter. All semblance of humour had escaped Bo's expression. The boy stared back at Fang with a wounded expression, twisted with hate. Raising his small fist, Bo flattened his fingers and palm and then sliced it across his neck, sticking his tongue out.

Kill the bastard.

Fang nodded, raising a clenched fist to

salute his new friend. The cloth wraps he'd wound about his own fist tightened in his grip, threads straining and snapping, the rigid muscles of his bicep and forearm coming into stark relief, fury manifest.

The two young men, one on the cusp of adolescence and the other barely years on the other side of the sea, shared this pact of vengeance, this thirst for deadly justice.

CHAPTER 12:

NIGHT OF KNIVES

Tony Woo was huffing and puffing from the sprint. The front of his open-collar ivory dress shirt was soaked with sweat, translucent and showing an array of chest hair.

"We... almost... there?" Woo whined, used to more close-quarters thumping and a whole lot less running.

"Yeah. You gonna puke, bitch?" Tai leered, elbows and knees pumping forward down the length of Tai Yau, towards the far end.

"Hahah.... hah!" Woo chuckled, stifling a gag. "Not as long as we get there in the next few goddamned minutes."

"Alright, alright," Tai slowed, growling. He raised his arm to signal a halt. "We need to take it a bit easier here on in. Only got a few bullets left and don't know if they got a gun on their Redpole. If they left any leaders behind we may have to save brass to take him out. Meantime, you need to catch your breath."

They were almost at the end of the dilapidated hallway that opened up into the Sun Ye On clubhouse. An informal arrangement, a moveable feast, a place that only existed in one space and at one time until it was ferreted out and destroyed, the Sun Ye On clubhouse was the first place the 14K family would have to search for Lin Ren.

A forest of overturned wicker baskets spilled out, covering the narrow hall, lacquered landmines. Stepping gingerly over the baskets, the gang attempted to catch their breath, Woo still having the worst of it. A black mass, they moved like snakes under flickering fluorescent lights, bundles of badly welded pipes, and burnt paper lanterns. It was like crawling down a nuclear bunker, bowing the head, minding the dripping water and chemicals, narrowing to a point of extremity. Not a soul lingered on the road. They passed a shoemaker, two bootleggers, a drug den, and finally a flower shop with busted blinds – still open – on the last leg of the journey. Finally, the 14K stared down a double-door, tin with wood reinforcement, painted with the image of a dragon.

Eerily quiet, Tai signaled a full stop. There was very little light here, the only source being a pair of cage lights, weak and covered with dust and the daily grime, flanking the wide doors. The men herded together.

"Gonna charge the door, burst through all at once. Weapons ready? Everyone good to go?"

"Caught up, boss. Ready to kick ass," Woo muttered, his thick frame hunkered down, chubby fingers thumbing the sharp edge of a long knife.

"Good here, Tai," Kwok said steadily.

"We gonna kill 'em? Or just cut 'em up a bit?" One of the initiates who had the luck to tag along tonight asked in a shaky whisper, afraid to trespass against the silence.

"Kill 'em, for fuck's sake!" Tai bellowed, raising his arm and voice in a battle cry, pushing himself from a squat into a full run for the doors. His men, his brothers and sons, came with him as a black-clad mass. Two thousand pounds of flesh and bone pierced the thin barricade of the double doors, splaying them wide, splintering the hasty wooden reinforcement the Sun Ye On had hastily constructed. Inside, their eternal foes were ready, weapons gripped in white-knuckled fists.

The common room turned to a tableaux of death. Tai stumbled, first in line, nearly catching himself jigged on the long point of a makeshift machete, a saw-blade strapped to a board. He batted the poor weapon aside, emptying two of the last four bullets into the would-be assassin. Blood spattered his face, ruby-red streams spraying from open wounds in the man's chest as he fell away from the father of the 14K. His men gained their footing soon afterward, though one unlucky bastard – the fresh-faced recruit that had asked the last question before they'd breached – found himself on the wrong end of a lead pipe. His skull opened up like a ripe melon from the two-handed blow; he crumpled to the floor, dead before he hit the ground.

Kwok found himself facing two mean mugging gangsters, one holding a metal baton and the other crouched in a martial arts stance. He knew it would be best to let them come at him at first, hopefully one at a time. Untrained fighters would come one at a time, without the risk of muddling each other's move – and this proved the case here. Swinging the baton clumsily, the Sun Ye On soldier stepped in, going for a crushing blow against Kwok's thigh, hoping to cripple the 14k enforcer. Kwok dodged the blow easily, stepping in behind the thug and slapping on a choke with effortless grace, the best way to disable a drunk tenant as well as a poorly trained enemy.

"Want me to break his fuckin' neck? You got five seconds to get your ass outta this room," Kwok shouted at the man moving back and forth in his stance. The man made no reply, made no move to exit, showed no concern for his ally. Kwok broke his captives neck in one smooth motion, slipping the baton into his own hand as his victim fell in front of him like a tipsy dance partner.

"So be it. Hope honour is worth death," Kwok grunted as he advanced on his opponent. The stoic opponent rose out of his low stance gracefully, aiming a fluid kick at Kwok's hand, striking true and flinging the baton from his possession. The metal struck a lantern hung from a nearby wall and shattered the shade, glass tinkling to the ground below as the melee raged on.

Woo's aviator sunglasses clacked noisily against the zipper of his leather jacket as he snapped and rolled to evade the blows of his own duet of opponents. Two men wielding switchblades darted at him, trying to sting him with their short blades, finding him much faster than his soft appearance belied.

Both men were tall and lean, almost twins, moving together and thinking alike, both dressed in dark leather jackets and denim jeans in poor condition. One of the twins reached out to stab Woo's protruding gut, the glittering edge of the blade catching the dark fabric of Woo's t-shirt and staying there, tangled up.

A master of aikido, Woo closed the short gap and immediately made short work of the Sun Ye On. His fat fingers wrapped around his rival's wrist, snapping it smoothly, then moving to grip his groin and throat, crushing both with incredible strength.

Tai thrust himself into the nearest group of Sun Ye On, his fists a blur, his teeth bared. He tore, ripped, punched, kicked, and scratched indiscriminately, like an iron-age berserker, searching for the secret of steel. His fingers caught the orbital socket of one young thug, he pressed into the soft tissue and popped the eyeball free, pulling it loose before delivering a dozen lethal elbows down on the nose, teeth, and finally the soft palate of his victim. Death would be a mercy for that man, an afterthought in Tai's consciousness as he sought new flesh to rend, new bones to break.

The Sun Ye On pushed back, forcing Woo into a corner, two dead soldiers at his feet. A rich looking luxury recliner pressed up against the wall next to him, buttoned upholstery holding in the interior like the strained button of Woo's dress shirt. Three men menaced him, until a young pup Tai had brought along cold-cocked one of them with a vicious haymaker, a perfect crescent that caught the outermost man on the temple, just below his greased sideburns, dropping him across the recliner and drawing the attention of the group. Woo and the young man stood shoulder to shoulder, facing the two that remained.

"Nice shot, son. Buy you a round or two when we get back!" Woo huffed, pushing off gracefully from his back foot and launching a front kick that caught his target in the midsection, driving deep into his guts. The young man at his side followed suit, attempting the same kick but finding himself caught in the grasp of his target. The Sun Ye On soldier twisted the young 14K's ankle, wrenching him to the ground, then scrambling to mount and choke him from the back, fingers flitting to reach for a hunting knife tucked into his waistband.

Without wasting time, Woo stepped forward, ignoring the threat of his own opponent, snatching the knife from the thug's waist and, with a dancer's pirouette, turning a full circle, arm extended. The blade caught his target kneeling, opening up an artery in his throat, lifeblood spraying like confetti about the small chamber. The remaining combatant attempted to rush Woo, who caught him with both arms and snapped his hips, releasing him in a full-momentum throw that saw the Sun Ye On sail across the room, crashing as a tangle of arms and legs into the remains of a homemade bar, all wood and glass splinters as the decanters and liquor bottles went flying.

The circle broke, then both sides stood apart, gauging their losses. Tai, Kwok, and Woo still stood, along with one of the new kids. A trio of fallen brothers lie broken at their feet. One unlucky 14K soldier struggled to breathe, coughing his lungs up, clutching a broken bar stool. The Sun Ye On were ragged, still reeling from the ambush at the central square and laundromat earlier, down a dozen. Both sides faced off, bloodied, bruised, torn by bites and clean cuts. Flesh hung loose at the irregular edges where skin and muscle had been ripped from bone. They looked like dead men, little difference between those prone and those still standing. The 14K outnumbered the Sun Ye On here, on their home turf, two to one. It was almost over.

"Impressive." Slow claps echoed about the destroyed room. An immaculately dressed gentleman of advanced age walked out of the far corner of the room. The percussive noise of his wrinkled palms was the source. He wore a sarcastic mask, punctuated by liver spots that covered the rest of his sunken face.

"Nianzu. Nice place you've got here," Tai hurled laconically, chest heaving. He gripped the spent pistol in reverse, finger wrapped in the trigger guard – improvised steel knuckles, the pistol whip. His hands were stained the colour of wine.

"Well, it was before you stupid bastards showed up. Barbarians... never know how to appreciate the finer things in life.

"Enough shit, Nianzu. Where's the girl? You tell me right now, politely, and maybe we don't have to kill you too. Just watch you scamper like the vermin you are out of this den, to never return."

"Well, see, here's the problem with that..." Nianzu drawled, both hands on the wide lapels of his chocolate brown suit. One hand reached down and pulled free a gleaming sidearm, almost twice the size of Tai's .38. The huge barrel of the gun stared down the leader of the 14K, Tai's mouth slackening in surprise. "... I don't think I want to run, after

214

all. At least, not without an apology for all the damage you've caused. Cash, if you please."

"Where the hell you get a piece like that?" Tai said.

"Why does it matter? All that matters is that I have a gun pointed straight at you. Pull the trigger, you're dead. Fit to toss in the pit with the rest of the bodies of all the scum that live here. Maybe *you* walk away, and maybe *you* never return, fucker."

"You think so? You pull the trigger and you die too. You think my word is that cheap? We said we were behind Fang and we are. This is about more than just Lin's life. It's about honour. Something you wouldn't know a damn thing about, Nianzu."

"Who cares about the girl? This whole city is over. This place will be nothing but a pile of concrete and scrap in a few years. Politicians want us all out. Cops want us all out. Matter of fact, they're going to retire nicely, too. Take a nice pension and enjoy the changing of the guard. Change... change is coming, Tai. Haven't you read the headlines? Will you let yourself and your brothers be swept away like dust? You will have nothing to show for it. The same as if you move against me now," Nianzu said, intensity radiating from him.

"Ah... the cops! That's where you got that

gun. That's where your loyalties lie. You're bought and paid for. A snitch. You just fucked up!" Tai pounced on the slip-up, the thread of lies.

"I wouldn't say – " Nianzu attempted to interject, pistol wavering as he saw Tai's strategy.

"And all those dead brothers of the Sun Ye On will have nothing to show for tonight's massacre. So too will these men…" Tai pointed the butt of his pistol at the handful of Sun Ye On soldiers still standing, flanking their boss, their father. "… die for a leader that cares nothing about them, ready to flee this so-called *hopeless city* with an even bigger cut!"

"Don't listen to him! He's 14K! Without honour!" Nianzu was fearful now, every word uttered urgently. He knew that living another day depended on it.

"Well, boys, I can tell you a few things. I can tell you that your father figure here, your own Redpole, didn't capture the girl for ransom against us, or Fang. He did it to cover some huge bets made by dirty cops. Fang throws the fight if we don't get Lin to safety. Big payout for the puppet, Nianzu here. Police stooge. If you die, he doesn't have to pay you. Ask your brothers, there…" he pointed to a gutted corpse, intestines loose.

216

He then pointed to a small, young man crumpled like a rag doll against the jukebox nearby, neat holes drilled through his chest. "...what they think about Nianzu's leadership. About his honesty. About his code of honour. He had that gun the whole time, hiding in the shadows, watching his portion grow with each one of you that fell on their sword for him."

Nianzu had already started taking a few steps backward, pulling the aim of the pistol from Tai, pointing it at the ground.

"You aren't really going to listen to Tai, are you? I have answers to everything! The girl isn't even back there!"

"Of course she's not, you snake!" Tai thundered, "You had her secreted away! You think these honourable brothers would die for an empty room? Hardly. But your new friends in the police force don't have the stomach for outright murder. Not where it concerns a prominent community figure like Fu Ren and his family. Rough her up a bit? Sure. Detain her for a bit? Sure. Blackmail her family to keep their mouths shut tonight and forever after? Sure. But not murder. She's too visible! Fu Ren would be furious and would have no reason left to keep your cover!"

One of Nianzu's men, squat and wearing a

stormy grimace, moved over to the door at the rear of the clubhouse. He produced a key from his pants pocket and fiddled with the lock. The door swung open; the Sun Ye On leaned in, scrutinizing.

"Girl's gone. Bindings on the floor. No sign of the guard," the short man reported. His eyes narrowed as did the rest of his remaining brothers. The Sun Ye On encircled their patriarch.

"Of course not!" Tai spat scornfully, "The guard was his man. Nianzu's hand-picked man, right? I bet he never showed his face, did he?"

The remnants of the Sun Ye On shook their heads in unison in the negative. Realization began to dawn on them, their suspicion palpable.

Nianzu was visibly shaken, not anticipating this turn of events, this power play, how Tai had cornered him, how his own family was turning on him.

"We bled for you. Died for you. For nothing? For your own greed and cowardice?" the short man intoned, barely flinching as Nianzu brought the gun to bear on him. Wordless judgment was passed between them, and like a mob of the living dead, they began to descend on their former father.

Nianzu screamed in fear and fury. The big handgun barked a half dozen times in quick succession, spinning a pair of men to the ground with grievous wounds. Then there were sick noises, like wolves at a feast. Then there was nothing but silence and a faint metallic scent mingling with the acrid smell of spent gunpowder.

A trio of Sun Ye On men were all that remained after the carnage. Theatrical, the scene was almost ethereal, the three betrayed bastards rising from their murder like demons, soaked in gore. Shredded into a dozen pieces, what was left of Nianzu resembled a macabre mosaic. The squat soldier was among them, and he produced the big handgun, no longer gleaming. Mechanically, the man checked the safety and then tossed it lightly towards Tai.

"Our lives are yours, father. Kill us for our sins, or release us to whatever fate may hold."

"Go, then," Tai said, "and never come back. Your lives are forfeit if you do."

"Our lives are over already. What has been done tonight cannot be undone. You have my thanks. May we never see one another again," the squat man said, bowing deeply. He and the other two survivors escaped the room, shutting the door behind them. Their eyes were glazed over and dull as they passed by the 14K.

Tai exhaled, all of the pent up tension of the last few minutes falling away from him, his frame falling. He popped the magazine from the butt of the bloody gun. Two bullets remained unfired. Nianzu's death had been too fast. A coward should die screaming for more than a few mere seconds, Tai thought to himself, especially when failing as spectacularly as he had in the eyes of his family.

"How did you know, boss?" Kwok said, limping over to stand at Tai's side.

"Soon as he mentioned the inevitability of the future, I knew he had strayed from the path. The gun was a solid-gold giveaway. Man like Nianzu spends his money on suits and pleasures of the skin, not hardware. Not here in Hong Kong; a gun here costs more than a hedonist is willing to part with – too much time away from his vices. Too many whores and highs could be bought for the same price. Cops are the only answer. They provide the piece for free to any traitor worth buying off. Seen it a few times."

Kwok nodded. It made sense to him. Memory jarred, Kwok recalled the loose and amateurish grip Nianzu had on the butt of the big pistol, a detail that had escaped scrutiny in the heat of the moment. This reinforced Tai's theory.

"So why fight at all? Why risk it with the Sun Ye On? He had to know that if they found out that this wasn't about leveraging us that they would kill him. A huge waste of resources," Kwok prodded.

"To stall us. To keep us away from the fighting pits. To keep us from protecting Fang, or from bringing Lin to him. Even now, we have no time to go to the Ren's home. It's still just a guess, Kwok. They could have killed her and disposed of the body. There's no way to be sure."

"So we lie to Fang? To get him to fight? Tell him Lin's fine, that she got away clean?"

Tai didn't answer, sliding the magazine back into place and pushing the safety off. He signaled for Kwok and Woo and the others to move out, double pace. The wounded trailed behind them, propped up over the shoulders of their sworn family.

They left behind a den of the dead, already beginning to stink of corruption, copper and sour.

CHAPTER 13:
THE WORLDS
BEST WARRIORS

The semifinals had already begun, and Yip had already tested Shuto's mettle. The Shaolin had scored a few heavy hits on Shuto, breaking the karateka's defenses and deadening his front leg, forcing Shuto to switch stances to protect his weakness. The crowd was zeroed into the action, nearly silent, the match an intense game of martial cat and mouse.

Shuto kept his feet planted, waiting for the Shaolin to move in on him; his defense was far too fluid for Shuto's style to effectively break the barrier. However, weak on offense, Yip dared much every time he entered Shuto's striking range. While both Shuto and the Shaolin were trained in patience and the importance of form, the karateka knew he could outlast the smaller man. He could sense a basic fear in Yip. Something only a lifelong predator could feel.

Hane had announced the fight with the usual flair. This time, satisfied by the first blood, the audience was more analytical, almost reserved. A hush had fallen amongst them, an invisible fog that dampened their vocal chords, yet stirred the heart. Fang could see some of the more empathetic attendees shaking with excitement. He had to admit that it was a glorious contest, like two vipers cast in a pit, darting in for the deathblow.

The navy blue of the platform was now so spotted with blood and sweat it resembled the midnight ocean, undulating beneath the footwork of the fighters. The torchlight that illuminated the room reflected the sheen of perspiration over their torsos. Yip had discarded the orange top of his two-piece uniform, fighting only in his loose-fitted pants, cinched at the ankle and at the waist with a simple black belt. Shuto fought in simple kickboxing shorts, eschewing the traditional gi. His mass alone was a psychological factor, muscles upon muscles, daring any to get too close.

223

Yip moved in, feinting to one side successfully, catching Shuto off guard. Leaping into the air, Yip threw a flying hook kick that caught Shuto across the skull, tumbling the man to the platform. Shuto shook it off, pushing himself back to his feet and clearing his vision. Yip smiled, then came again, this time feinting to the other side. Shuto saw the Shaolin telegraph this move, and was there when Yip least expected it, appearing in front of him. Shuto rammed his fist into Yip's gut, following up with a vicious combination of jabs and elbows that battered the Shaolin's face. Finishing the combination off with a textbook front kick that doubled Yip over, Shuto backed off to a safe distance to appraise the damage.

Yip had one hand draped along the ridges of his chest, gurgling. He retched, bile streaming from between his lips flecked with something darker. With his free hand, he wiped his mouth clean, then retreated to the far edge of the platform. He did not re-enter fighting position. Shuto began to advance, a shark. He declined to drop his guard, sensing a ruse.

Shuto was correct; Yip regained his edge a moment before Shuto could close the gap, the light returning to his eyes. Shuto tried a leg sweep, thick thighs powering forward; Yip jumped lightly over the sweep and grappled Shuto's guard arm, wrenching it harshly and tossing the larger man end over end. Before Shuto could regain his footing, the Shaolin was on him, going for the same arm, bracketing his legs overtop Shuto's chest and face, beginning an armbar.

Yip was unable to get enough torque to lock the hold in. Shuto's massive arms were too strong, even now the karateka was beginning to lift Yip clear of the canvas. Yip kicked out with his heel smashing it into Shuto's skull. Growling with anger, Shuto rolled over, slamming Yip hard into the platform after having lifted him up, now atop the smaller man.

Yip had broken Shuto's nose, a crimson river flowing from both nostrils, down across the broad jaw, onto the neck. This didn't stop the fighter-for-hire from manhandling the Shaolin now. Shuto straddled his opponent and struck him again and again mercilessly. His fists were hammers upon an anvil, coming down with such violence that the very first drove all sense from Yip, knocking him unconscious. The rest were murder, crushing the bones of the man's skull, driving splinters of what used to be Yip's face into Shuto's knuckles. The sight of exposed bone and the thick arcs of blood that flew from Shuto's fists as he raised them and then brought them down time and again caused the crowd to roar their assent.

In the interminable seconds that came after, Shuto continued his murderous assault, until finally he felt the grasping hands of the referee pulling at his shoulders. Shuto shook the hands free effortlessly, returning to his work. Now there was nothing left of Yip's face, the front of his skull beaten in like a rotten fruit. The mob was orgasmic, enthralled. This is what they had paid to see. A gore soaked titan, his muscles rippled as he brought death to his foe with his bare hands. It was a spectacle as old as the human race, a thrill as old as time.

Now a strange wall of arms and hands hauled Shuto from atop his victim. He frothed, grinding his teeth and spitting. His focus was on returning the pain he had suffered a hundredfold, his vanity and narcissism manifest.

"Hey! Hey! Snap out of it!" the referee and the ring attendants shouted in his ear, attempting to calm the beast. Flagging torches illuminated the still body of the Shaolin. Shuto began to come back to his body, his spirit returning from another plane. His face and fists ached; he looked down through blurred vision as a red mist lifted from his vision. Bits of bone mixed in with the blackness of drying blood. He saw the hands wrapped about his chest and neck and tossed his head from side to side, trying to place himself in time and space.

The referee, confident that the other three attendants had Shuto in restraint, circled around to face the frenzied fighter. He leaned in, shining a small pen-light into Shuto's face. He reached a hand in and peeled back Shuto's eyelid. Shuto could feel his fingers shaking against his forehead. He laughed deliriously, like a madman.

"Questionable concussion, broken nose," the referee spoke into his ear, also for the benefit of the attendants, "He can continue. Get the body out of here, to the back." He waved the attendants off before straightening up, beckoning Hane up on stage to announce the winner before the pop of the mob was extinguished, wanting to keep emotions running high. It was great for business.

Hane complied, scrambling onto the stage and reaching out to grab at the microphone which once again dropped down, almost knocking him in the face. Awkwardly palming it and then snapping it on, Hane began his speech, Shuto being helped to his feet by the men who had been wrestling with him moments earlier. The referee made a quick exit, smoothly exiting the stage, heading straight for the spiral staircase leading to the crow's nest, where the officials would pass judgment.

The rabble was coming down from their high, some showing regret on their faces as they watched the mangled corpse of the dead fighter dragged unceremoniously from the edge of the platform. Hane himself couldn't help but to hazard a quick look before spinning about, one arm in the air, the other holding the mesh of the mic to his lips.

"Ladies and gentlemen! What a sight to behold! What a show! We should not cry for Yip, we should honour him. He fought well. All men who enter this square tonight know that their lives are on the line! What good is a contest if the wages for failure are too little? What laurels can we award a champion that does not have another man's blood on his hands?"

Fang thought Hane might be overdoing it with the monologue, but he said nothing. His attention was bound up by the reaction of his father, and his friends, appearing worrisome in the uppermost rows of the stands opposite him.

Cai Shi's skin was almost translucent, white like a specter. Both Yu and Mei, flanking his father, looked sickly. Fang could feel their anxiety, could feel fear begin to grip him, to take hold of his chi. He strangled these feelings, forcing them into an interior void. He would need all of his courage and wit to withstand Bai, to last long enough to know the truth about what fate had befallen Lin. He ran his fingers through his hair, waiting for Hane to finish. It may have been Fang's imagination, but he thought he saw Hane wink at him as he concluded his remarks.

"Now, friends, only two fights remain. Three men are left standing, and only two will enter the final round. Until then, however, we'll have to take a short intermission to clean the ring and to confer with the official judges on whether a disqualifying penalty for forcefulness will be issued to last bout's victor."

At this a caterwaul came from the men in the stands, boos and hisses. Then Fang saw him – Captain Tong. Outside of his usual uniform of course, Tong bore little resemblance to the man Fang had faced off against in the interrogation room. His neat shirt and ironed slacks were replaced by shoddy, wrinkled clothing that blended in with the scavenged garments common to the underclass gathered here tonight. Only a few big shots and high rollers in the front rows were wearing anything better, suit jackets and blazers ill-balanced against the great unwashed.

Tong's attention was fixed on the officiants' booth, his eyes never leaving the trio of men huddled together in conversation. Tong touched an earpiece, barely visible, wrapped about his left ear. Fang's suspicions were aroused. After a few spoken words, Tong looked visibly perturbed, smoothing out his clothing unconsciously. Then Fang lost him as the mob shifted in the stands, Tong moving away from his perch and others floating by in a desperate hunt for their beer and a fix.

Cops in the walled city? Cops competing in the kumite? The foundations of Fang's world were shaken. Even his personal penchant for black humour couldn't overcome the uneasy feeling that things weren't exactly going his way tonight. He felt his focus begin to waver; Bai stood up and started flicking his hands, clenching and unclenching his fists, jaunting from side to side in warmup.

A few minutes of intense deliberation passed, the short judge wearing the same robe as the dead competitor arguing vehemently with the other two, gesticulating angrily, his words failing to reach the ears of anyone beyond the booth. One thing was clear, the crow's nest was still in confusion as to how to resolve the problem of such clear murder; this was no accidental death. Yet a penalty of any sort would throw off all the odds, and would be unenforceable in any fair contest – further, a true champion could not be crowned if a finalist was outright barred from competition for their methods in a full-contact contest, even if those methods were in dispute with the spirit of the Siu Nin a Fu.

A cloud still hanging over him, glowering, the short Shaolin officiant relented, sitting down in his chair and closing his eyes, fingers massaging his temples. The other two judges calmly returned to their own seats, eyes scanning the crowd. The referee, relieved, scuttled down the stairs hurriedly and returned ringside, cupping a hand and whispering into Hane's ear. Hane nodded, stonefaced. He plastered on a stagecraft smile and vaulted back onto the platform, twirling theatrically. His microphone descended with practiced ease.

"The judges have spoken! A verdict has been rendered! The contest will continue!"

The rude roar of the crowd returned, renewed and invigorated by the taste of cold beer and fresh hits floating through the veins.

Bai stepped onto the platform, and as he did so, a cascade of boos crashed down upon him. He sneered at the slurs and insults thrown at him, and spat through the hole in this teeth.

"Returning to the ring, fresh from his thrilling win over the legendary Otomo... the Bull!" Hane kept it short this time, not wanting to interrupt the catcalling of the crowd. Bai simply began stretching on his side of the platform, paying no heed.

"And of course, fine residents of Kowloon Walled City, no contest within these walls would be complete without our rising star, our favourite son. Iron Fang Shi!" Hane extended his arm, fingers splayed, towards Fang. Hane's suit was starting to wrinkle, his hair starting to droop, the humidity in the room soaring as the night wore on. He was starting to resemble a jester rather than a professional ring announcer, a sense of the carnivale began to creep in, incorporating itself into the many sins of the evening.

Fang tightened the wraps about his fists, testing them, flexing his hands and feeling the thin cotton tight against his knuckles. The chants grew louder, rhythmic. He slowly stood and took his place opposite Bai, frozen. He let no emotion show, cladding his chi in the focus that years of training and street-fighting had taught him. Bai, on the other hand, danced about, trying to shake off the injuries of his scrap with the sumo.

"Fight!" Hane called in tandem with the sounding of the gong, stepping smoothly off the skirt of the ring onto the ground.

Fang stepped in immediately, fists moving in a blur, jabs striking through Bai's guard like soft butter. The Bull's head was snapped back, sweat flying from his bald head. A swift sweep of the leg caught the bigger man off-guard, tumbling him free of the platform onto the ground. Laughter rippled from the crowd as Bai stood up, dusting himself off, grimacing at Fang.

"Supposed to make it look good," said Fang in a stage-whisper to his opponent, corners of his mouth tugging upward as the referee directed them to starting positions.

With a cutting motion, the ref returned them to hostilities and the two fighters circled one another. This time, Bai's guard was much higher, his forearms a wall before his thick neck and face.

Fang moved in again, low, feinting at a mid-section assault before straightening up for another jab to the face. This time Bai caught him, a loose right cross from the big man catching Fang across the jaw, hurling him to the ground. The bull rushed forward, driving a heel downward in a hard stomp; Fang rolled away and sprang back to his feet, brushing a lock of black hair away from his face.

"Close one, kid," Bai said. He slurred the words, the damage to his mouth deforming his speech.

Now it was Bai's turn to mount an offensive. Forgetting the bum-rush, this time the undercover cop tried a more deliberate approach, spreading his stance and crab-walking towards Fang, fencing the smaller man into a corner where Bai's reach could take advantage. Seeing the ploy, Fang moved in to prevent the closing of the trap, sailing off a side snap kick that caught Bai in the ribs.

Bai grunted in pain but did not slow, nor double over. Instead, thick hands caught Fang's ankle, wrenching it over and flipping the younger man to the ground on his stomach, winding him. Kicking out desperately with his heel, Fang managed to break the hold, but before he could stand, Bai managed to catch him with a spiteful football kick that caught him in the thigh, rolling him onto his back.

Bai moved to straddle Fang; instead the spirited soldier of the 14K managed to once again kick out with his heel, catching Bai full in the gut, pushing through the thin abdominal muscles. This time Bai did succumb, jack-knifing and gasping. Fang fought to a kneeling position, then standing. Before Bai could fully recover, Fang tried another kick, putting his faith in his weaker leg, hoping the numbness was not a symptom of something more serious. He could feel the burn in his thigh as his other leg launched outward, catching Bai again in the ribs, the same place as before. The Bull staggered back a few paces from the blow, his hands pressing against the new wound instead of forming a guard.

"Remember the deal, you little shit!" Bai hissed between broken teeth. Fang could see Tong over Bai's shoulder, piercing the veil of combat, breaking Fang's focus. Tong's eyes were dark, glinting like a viper, as he drew his folded fingers across his throat, reminding Fang of his threat.

"Time to fall down, little boy," Bai said, barreling forward.

Fang entered a world of pain at Bai's hands. Returning Fang's favour earlier, Bai's punches landed all over Fang's face, breaking his distracted guard and catching him on the jaw, the nose, the mouth. Blood burst from his mouth as his teeth cut his lips to shreds. He felt himself folding under the barrage, the taste of iron against his tongue. Fang clung to consciousness by a thread.

Bai stepped back and set to deliver his finisher, a spinning roundhouse. Fang's guard was weak, barely there. Time seemed to move like a turgid river for Fang, ghostly images presenting themselves in his mind.

He saw Bai's mangled visage, twisted with hate. He saw the leg cock back, the hip turning on a fulcrum, building force. He saw the torches dotting the inky blackness, like faerie fire.

He saw Lin, standing next to her father, the fire reflected in her eyes. Her father stood stock-still next to her, inscrutable.

Bai launched his roundhouse, screaming with ferocity that matched the intent of his finishing move. Fang's shaky guard caught Bai's shin like a dam made from twigs against a tsunami, and was washed away. Bai's leg followed through, the shinbone striking Fang across the temple and tossing him, spinning through the air, to the mat. A thick coil of black blood sluiced from between his lips, staining the ring and the ground beyond, splashing against the feet of those in the first row. Cai Shi, Mei, and Yu looked on in horror from the top of the stands. Their hearts sank as one.

"Fang!!!" Lin cried out, her face ugly with grief. Her words reached out across a great chasm of unconsciousness. Fang's head lolled side to side, his chest barely moving. Bai raised his arms in defiance of the denizens of the walled city. A hail of scrap paper, sore loser's betting sheets, showered down upon him, some sticking to his glistening shoulders. The boos of the crowd began to die off as the realization that their champion had been felled sank in, weighing deeply on them all. The torches themselves seemed to dim. The balls of soiled rags and oil shrank against fate.

Tai, flanked by Kwok and Woo, pushed their way into the stands. Seeing their brother down, defeated, broke them. The trio of men wailed in unison. Their grief was palpable. All of their sacrifices had been for nothing.

"Get the hell up, Fang!" Tai called out, bellowing in fury and disbelief. "She's safe! She's here! *She loves you! We love you!*"

His words caught the ear of some of the men nearby, who craned about to stare at the newcomers with disbelief. Tai and his lieutenants were caked in gore themselves, the look of men who have gone running through the alleys with knives looking for bad fortune and found it.

"Fang! Fang! Fang!"

First it was his father, Cai Shi. He was shaking like a leaf in the wind. Then it was Mei, her pretty face drained of all colour. Then it was Yu, his surrogate brother, enflamed. Then it was the rest of his adoptive family. Then it was the entire crowd. At first a whisper, then a scattered sentiment, then rising like a phoenix from the ashes of a forlorn hope.

Fang heard his name. His eyes snapped open. He saw the pinpricks of light, low-slung and sparse. He heard Lin's voice. She was here. She was safe. Fang rolled over onto his hands and knees, grimacing as clotted bile fell from between his clenched teeth.

Hane stretched a hasty arm across the chest of the referee who had begun to enter the ring to call the fight as being over.

Bai's back was to Fang; he had joined in the cheering of the crowd for their champion, his expression one of exultant, twisted mockery. Behind his back, Fang managed to take a knee, his forearm resting atop. Fang spat a web of phlegm and blood beyond the narrow ring apron. He steadied himself, re-aligning his focus. He turned his head to look at Lin, reassuring himself that she was really here and not a phantom.

Their eyes met, and locked together. Hers were filled with suffering, though her bruises from being held in the interrogation room seemed to have largely healed. Her captors hadn't hurt her since. Her small hands were folded atop her breasts. Fu Ren stood beside her, his expression frosty. Cold as ice, he stared at Fang with unbridled disgust. It was clear that he was not here of his own volition. Lin had obviously made an impassioned plea to be here, beside Fang tonight. Fang looked back to Lin with the thin shadow of a smile, grotesque, earnest.

Bai had by now figured out that something was amiss, for the crowd had crowned another king, calling out the name again and again of the man he had left in tatters at his back. Pivoting about, he saw Fang in a crouch, shaking his head. Bai could not contain his great surprise, even taking a short step backward in horror. No man could have survived the vicious blow Bai had visited upon him.

"Seems like back-alley losers are harder to kill than I imagined!" Bai growled, getting over his shock and raising both hands, like claws. He slowly advanced on the downed Fang, fingers reaching for a stranglehold to

crush the life from Fang's throat. Fang knew
he only had one chance to seize opportunity.

Powering up from his crouch, and using
both arms to split Bai's guard aside, Fang
snapped his skull upward, catching Bai with
a brutal reverse headbutt that slammed the
cop's jaw shut with an audible crunch.
Canines and incisors bit through the soft
tissue of the tongue, severing it entirely. Bai
shrieked, gurgling like an infant, the loose
folds of flesh that had been his tongue fell
free of his mouth.

Fang stayed close, delivering hard elbows
to the midsection he had been working
earlier, each strike harder than the last. He
could feel the momentum shifting, the
energy fleeing Bai's body as he broke his
ribs, feeling them splinter against his
forearm. Fang kept punishing the cruel bull,
sweeping his skinny legs out from underfoot
as the crowd built to a climax. They
observed, enraptured, as the small
streetfighter fell heavily atop the much
larger man, short punches seeking the same
bruised spot below Bai's arm.

Bai rolled about, thrashing wildly,
screeching in anger and in desperation,
spitting pieces of his cheek and tongue in a
fine mist of vermillion. His large stature had
failed him, his techniques not enough to

conquer the spirit of the younger, hungrier Fang. A great and irregular island was the bruise beneath his left arm, a constellation of shattered ribs and blood vessels. He choked, gagging. His eyes bulged, bloodshot. Moving upwards in the one-sided clinch, Fang caught Bai across the face with a clean right cross, and then it was over. Bai was unconscious.

The very foundation of Kowloon Walled City shook with the sound of Fang's victory. His name echoed from the wooden pillars that held the limitless night above them all. The breath of those who had fought with him vicariously nearly extinguished the dying light cast by the fading oil of the torches. He fell back on his ass, propped up on a scabrous palm, trying to catch his breath.

The referee flung himself into the ring, scrambling hand over foot to reach Bai's side. Checking his pulse, he seemed to nod a slight sigh of relief at finding faint vitals.

"Roll him onto his side or he'll choke like the dog he is." Fang rasped, chest heaving. His long locks were matted, wet, to the nape of his neck and about his slight collarbone. The referee complied, placing the back of his palm against Bai's nose to ensure his airway was clear. Satisfied, he stood and motioned for Fang to take his hand.

"Fang Shi! Fang Shi! Fang Shi! Fang Shi!" the two syllables thundered over them both. Fang caught Hane's eye as the referee grasped his fist and thrust it into the air, sending the fans into a frenetic dance. The dapper Japanese expatriate simply nodded in reply, repeating his wink from earlier. The familiar wink reminded Fang of something.

Removing his fist from the victory pose, reclaiming it as his own, Fang spun about the platform, looking for her. He saw his father, tears streaming down his aged face. He saw Mei and Yu, hugging each other in the throes of joy. He saw his brothers, and Tai, stern pride reflected in them all as they stood tall and alone aside from the wooden risers. He saw Captain Tong, face contorted with an ugly, unreadable emotion, speaking hysterically into his earpiece. He saw Shuto, whose face was carved from iron, focused and far away.

He did not see Lin, nor her father.

CHAPTER 14:
THE KNIFE HAND

The intermission had been set at a full half hour; this was amenable to all parties.

It gave time for Fang to recuperate, shaking sore hands with his fans as well as his family and friends. No matter what happened now, he had proven himself a true warrior in their eyes, a champion of his people.

It gave time for Shuto to exit his trance, all semblance of his sarcastic demeanour drowned beneath a professional exterior. He was practicing his forms, textbook perfect, in the middle of the platform. Each motion was a work of art, a transference of knowledge from times and lives that died long ago.

It gave time for the rest of them to get blackout drunk and high, rowdy and set to full blast. Wagers were made non-stop, a hive of hands reaching for coloured chips and crudely stenciled pieces of paper. Coins rang out against one another, high and tinny. Broken beer bottles sounded like little laughing chimes, glass bouncing against wood, steel, and cement. As ever, no noise escaped the overseer's booth, the men leaning back in their seats casually and, for the first time, looking relaxed.

Like all moments after spent passions, a lull of peace persisted afterward. A bubble, a barrier, a threshold of time that marked the passage between states of being, between ultimate glory and eternal shame. A constant, manic buzz was present, building to another climax.

Then it was time. Total silence draped over the room for a span of heartbeats. Then a cough. A whistle. Then insults, encouragements, and advice from afar. A slow, babbling brook of murmurs, indistinct.

Hane stood between the two men. He'd had plenty of time to sharpen up his look and now he was wound up tight. The strut was back in his stride as he made small circles in the center of the platform. Swinging his arms, the mic and cable whipping about like a jump-rope, Hane waited for the murmuration to build to a full roar, then cut in with his slick, strong crooning: "One last time! One final fight! One man left standing! Men and women of Kowloon Walled City, here in the heart of Hong Kong, the birthplace of legends! … Are you ready to go – one last time!?!"

Hane's magic worked; the throng ate it up, ravenous. Their desire exploded, fists pumping in the air, howls and catcalls mingling in the encroaching darkness. Hane continued.

"To my left! A man who needs no introduction, knocking all comers aside as if they were child's playthings – toys for his amusement. And just like toys, Shuto broke them and tossed them aside..."

The tasteless reference did not seem so odious to those hanging on Hane's every word; the pun drew a few gasps that were crushed under the gales of rough laughter.

"... and found himself facing the survivor. The streetfighter. The man who had no name, and found one here. At first in the narrows, the labyrinth where he conquered Li Zhao. The city where so many fell in front of him, never to rise to claim their own names. And tonight, he has a name."

The mob spoke it for him, as one, some swaying on their feet drunkenly. The chant of his name filled Fang with a surge of pride, secure in the knowledge that his honour and his name were both intact. Now a single obstacle remained, a final stain against Fang's reckoning. He wished Lin remained to witness him at the height of his glory.

Fang's scars seemed to shine in what was left in the light cast from the smoldering sconces. Still wet with sweat and blood, his already dark hair looked the colour of coal. His muscles, dotted with wounds, nonetheless stood out in sharp relief against his slender frame. Shuto's physique told a starkly different tale. His bronzed skin seemed smooth, relatively undamaged, though his face had seen better days. His stance was high, studious, and formal in contrast with Fang's looser street-fighting stance. Fang knew that he had no hope against the mercenary karateka with one style alone.

Both men's faces were a ruinous mess of cuts, swelling, and broken bones. Despite this, they held frame, shoulders facing, guards up.

"BEGIN!" Hane cried, not bothering to wait for the referee. The gong, startled, sounded off. The erratic start didn't seem to faze either man, both patiently awaiting their chance.

The men rushed each other immediately,

locking up in the middle of the ring. Fang slammed his knees into Shuto's stomach, trying to break through the big man's rock-hard abdominals. They held against his assault, sapping energy from Fang. In the interim, Shuto had managed to grip Fang by his shorts, about the hips, lifting him into a deep suplex. The two bodies arced, the move perfection, Shuto slamming Fang down on the edge of the platform. Fang groaned and writhed on the edge of the ring, one arm falling over the edge, curses coming from the crowd.

"I still make money, and you all still go home poor nobodies!" Shuto remarked, shouting at the stands as he stood. The boos doubled in number, as did the size of his lopsided smirk. He waved them off and set to gripping Fang by the shoulders, kneeling to wrap a thick forearm and bulging bicep about Fang's small neck.

Fang felt the thick limbs encircle him, immediately locking in like a vice. His legs dangled freely over the edge of the platform, unable to find any purchase. Black whorls of ink joined otherworldly colours exploding before his eyes. Imagining a boa constrictor smothering its prey, Fang fought weakly against the sleep.

He thought of his father's face, once alight

with pride, falling ashen and grey, then fading away.

He thought of Lin, her look of love, of fright, of horror. Then she, too, faded away.

He thought of Tai, and Mei, and Yu, and the others. They came to him as fuzzy figures, ghosts, scattered in their arrangement. His thoughts scattered to the four winds.

He thought of Bo. He thought of lit cigarettes and the oblivion of cheap whiskey. The bar.

He thought of the trick he learned at the bar, in his first barfight.

Big man had young Fang in a deathgrip. Couldn't have been more than fourteen or so. Tried to stick up for Mei when a group of drunk toughs had wanted to make something more of their service than simple flirting. He'd taken two of them out, but the fat man had hit him with a beer bottle when he wasn't looking, then slapped on a sloppy chokehold. Fang was fading fast, the man's sordid breath blowing down hot on his face.

"His ears, Fang! His ears!" Mei called out to him. Years of being a petite girl tending bar in the depths of Hak Nam, the city in the dark, had taught her some survival skills.

Fang clapped his hands against the big man's ears with as much strength as he could muster. He felt the choke break away, and he rolled away, coughing, whooping for air. Fang could hear his attacker a few feet away, crying out in pain.

Fang glanced over to see Shuto clutching his ears, fingers trying to dig out an invisible hurt.

Still wretching, lungs rattling, Fang stumbled over to Shuto and leveraged a clumsy football kick into the mercenary's chest, knocking him flat. Shuto's hand reached out, grasped Fang's ankle, and pulled one of his legs out from under him, felling him to the canvas as well.

Both men crawled towards one another, grappling each other in counterbalance as they attempted to gain their footing, trading blows. Fang dodged more than he sustained, though those that did land home hurt him badly. Shuto was struck again and again and again by Fang's true aim, quick blows that disoriented him and opened the previous wounds on his face. Breaking contact, Fang backpedaled to a safe distance and massaged his throat, keeping one eye on the only enemy he had left in the world.

"Last two fights took a lot out of you, boy." Shuto exhaled, dropping down to back stance, *kokutsu dachi*, placing his weight on his back leg and hunkering down. He wanted to bring Fang into his reach.

"Still have enough left to deal with a coward. A coward who beats women," Fang growled weakly, his voice threatening to abandon him.

Shuto laughed without breaking eye contact, still circling. His footfalls were silent. Fang kept his feet moving, boxing style, looking for any break he could get to reach in, and reach out.

"You should be thanking me, boy. Wasn't your boys that took Lin home. I brought your pretty little girl back to her father. Tonight. Not before having a little fun first, though," Shuto leered. He swapped his back stance so that his right leg was now facing forward and his left hand was cocked at the hip.

"You lie!" Fang spat, strafing in on Shuto. Dodging Shuto's lunge punch, Fang caught Shuto with a good hook, snapping the karateka's head back. He caught a little bit of Shuto's counterpunch on his guard and backed out of range.

"Lucky shot, kid. The truth piss you off? No more talking." Shuto transitioned into the more aggressive front stance.

"Looking for a big finish? The truth might piss me off, but it fucking scares you!" Fang cried, his eyes flashing. Sprinting forward, angling himself, Fang leapt into the air well above Shuto's guard. His leg shot out, the ball of his foot catching Shuto in the throat, collapsing his windpipe.

Shuto's hands shot to his neck, fingers probing his throat frantically. He sank to his knees, tearing at the flesh of his neck. Like an executioner, Fang moved in, accompanied by the exultation of his fanatics.

A hard right hook across the face, followed by a vicious back elbow from the same arm across the bridge of an already broken nose. Shuto's strangled shriek was caught in his throat, a pathetic noise.

"No more talking." Fang reminded his opponent. He watched the tower of bone and muscle that was the defeated karateka fall limp to the mat in front of him.

The silence returned, a spell cast over the room. Now, almost entirely extinguished, the slight flames left burning in the sconces resembled embers in a cast-iron stove, black with soot. Fang stood over Shuto – and every man here had borne witness.

Shuto did not stir, his flesh immobile.

Fang felt a warm hand on his shoulder, a friendly squeeze that nonetheless pained his bruised flesh.

"Ladies and gentlemen, families, fathers and sons, mothers and daughters... I present to you all... tonight's victor..."

They hung on Hane's every word. Fang's head drooped, but he was smiling, unseen, to himself. He reached out with an unsteady hand to rest upon Hane's padded shoulder. The blood would match the blazer anyways, Fang noted, his wry grin widening in secret, obscured by shadows.

"...and the new *Champion* of Kowloon Walled City, 1984 ... FANG SHI!" Hane announced, drawing out every syllable, allowing the sound of Fang's victory to linger, to touch every nook and cranny of the dank tournament chamber where light dared never tread.

Fang shut his eyes. He let the adulation in. He let himself believe, for once, that he was more than just a loser from the rotten corpse of a dying city. He believed in the image that others saw when they looked at him.

Then there was a cold feeling, a sharp pain like melting icewater, deep in his gut. He looked down to see a short blade protruding from his side, black trails already running freely. A numbness spread from his waist outward. Fang fell over awkwardly, his bandaged hands pressing against the base of the knife to stop the bleeding.

Someone was crying his name. Someone was streaking down from the bleachers in a blur, their motion soft around the edges.

Fang's exhaustion and injury combined to push him towards the shores of sleep. His heart told him to close his eyes, and he did. They were heavy, much too heavy, to lift alone.

CHAPTER 15.

MEMORY

OF A MOMENT

Fang slowly worked his hand against hers, taking in every fold of her skin. She squeezed back, gently. It still hurt; the doctor said it would hurt for a month yet, maybe two.

He'd spent a week in the hospital – the real one, the one with electricity that wasn't stolen and tools of the newest surgical steel. Part of his winnings, she'd told him. She'd visited him every day, bringing a new bouquet of fresh flowers each morning. He often looked at them, admiring the arrangements. One day, lilies, the colour of sunset. The next, orchids, the colour of a lake under a full moon. She had a very romantic

254

heart, one that could forgive mistakes and forget the past.

Yu had visited him, along with Tai and the rest of his brothers. Tai clutched the hollow aluminum rails of his hospital bed, hovering over him, inspecting his face. Yu told the tale of what had transpired.

A sneaky little man, barely in his twenties, had crept near the platform and planted the knife in Fang's gut before anyone had time to react. Attempting to flee, he'd been turned on by the crowd. The mob had penned him in and beaten him ruthlessly until he was nothing but dismembered limbs – one less loose end for Fang and the family.

That wasn't the end of the savage night, however.

Whispering into his ear, Tai told him of how he'd caught Captain Tong making a quick exit of the city. Tong hadn't made it. Tai had taken a cheap boat tour of Kowloon Bay the next day, leaning against the railing of the lower deck, nonchalantly dropping the big handgun he'd been gifted by Nianzu's defectors into the deepest part of the water. Despite the great value of the piece, no sum was worth the risk of being caught and convicted a cop-killer. Tong's body was filled with the bullets from the gun he'd handed to his own double-crossing bastard and would match to no known weapon in Hong Kong.

Tai knew the news would make Fang happy. The circle was whole, all challengers burned away.

Yu had thought to bring him Viola's breakfast, double bacon. Again, part of the winnings, they told him. Fang wondered aloud just how large the purse had been. Everyone had told him not to worry about it; just worry about getting better.

"That big, huh?" He'd told them.

They just smiled and told him it wasn't about the money. It was.

His father visited him. He had a pack of the expensive smokes crumpled up in the pocket of his sweater. A sweater with no holes in it from mould or from cigarette burns. His share of the winnings, his father had said, a twinkle in his eye. Fang had never felt closer to him. They spoke of his mother, and their mutual love for her – this time without anxiety or shame. Cai Shi told his son that his mother may not have been there to watch him earn his name, but that she would have been proud of him. That they were *both* proud of him.

Now, though, in the days that came after – Fang was holding her hand as they walked down the length of Lo Yan, past Yeung's, headed for the outside. He still walked with a limp, but that would subside over time as the stiffness abated – or the drugs kicked in, whichever.

Then the walled city was at their back. It was late afternoon, both he and she had to shade their eyes against the sapphire skyline; not a cloud in the sky. Looking back, Fang spied two figures waving from the rooftop. Young Bo and the drunkard Liu stood side by side, waving enthusiastically to the couple. Bo formed a horn with his hands and placed them to his mouth, hollering something down to the two of them. The sonic whine of jet engines drowned away all hope of hearing Bo's message, a descending passenger plane buzzing the building for the first time this afternoon. A flurry of wings, coloured in every hue of the rainbow, flourished behind the unlikely duo. Liu and Bo laughed at the startled birds, knowing they would return.

Fang laughed with them, regardless of having heard the message or not, and waved the two fools off. The odd pair, forty years apart and yet bearing fast friendship, was effortlessly endearing.

She told Fang how happy she was that they could finally leave the walled city. She told him how relieved she was to see him walking again and improving every day. Every word she spoke to him cried love. Fang felt the same way; he would do anything for her. She hadn't fled from his side when things had gotten deadly serious. That was a crucible from which very few lovers escape whole.

Deep into December, the streets were flooded with people reading newspapers. The news was saying that Hong Kong, Kowloon included, the walled city included – was going to be handed back to China. Not today, not tomorrow, but someday. A gradual process, like erosion. Fang never paid much attention to politics, and neither did she. Still, it was impossible to ignore the rumblings and the uncertainty.

The news dwindled little in their minds as they walked hand in hand through the bustling streets of downtown Hong Kong. Holiday decorations were spraypainted on signs; bunting hung from the clotheslines strung from window to window far out of reach. Some nights a cold wind, the feathers of a monsoon, would cast a slight chill. Today there was no such threat, with most people wearing jeans and a loose t-shirt or thin sweater.

The pressures of the shopping season meant that traffic was now bumper to bumper, and they moved faster on foot than most motorists as they strolled along at their leisure.

The place next to the Rare Petal, the Meadows, was a place she'd never been before. Fang, a bit more worldly, led the way. They kissed outside the doors; he pulled her slim waist against his, running his strong fingers up and down her back. Her lips sought his hungrily. They both pushed one another away gently, looking for the light in each other and finding it returned.

They walked into the reception area at the Meadows. She loved it; it was such a fleeting treat to leave the confines of the concrete maze they called home. A well dressed, well kept host seated them, a pair of warm towels for their laps draped over his arm. The menu was extensive and exquisite, advertised in bold letters that brooked no qualm about the quality of the chef and his craft. The table linens were of a rich purple, the colour of velvet pansies, with jade piping. A steel bucket of spirits, rice wine, and domestic beer mixed with crushed ice was placed centrally, chill perspiration sinking into the plush fabric of the tablecloth, turning it black. The waiter was impeccable, every word a gentleman, and he took their order without error.

"I really appreciate this. You don't really have to do all of this for me," she said, embarrassed. She was fidgeting despite her smart blouse and pants, something she'd borrowed from her mother.

"You deserve it. You saved my life," Fang said. He reached his hand out to caress her cheek. She closed her eyes and nuzzled against his palm for a moment, reaching up to cup the back of his hand with her own. Slight fingers played with his busted knuckles. Her long dark hair cascaded like a waterfall over his fingers, slightly ticklish.

"It wasn't a choice, Fang. It wasn't a choice." She shook her head from side to side, gazing intently at him. She gently moved his hand between hers on top of the table.

Their food arrived shortly thereafter. Fang's noodles and beef with a side of curry was steaming hot, herbs making his mouth water. She'd decided to try something new, and brushing her bangs aside, set to popping pieces of fried chicken and shrimp into her mouth.

Now they drank, Fang trying the liquor, then the wines, then finally nursing his beers. She drank glass after glass of red wine, a robust Italian. They flirted, and joked, and laughed. The other diners made their exit while she and Fang stayed. Eventually it was time to leave; the restaurant was closing, though their large bill and even larger tip guaranteed a friendly parting.

As their footfalls rang out on the sidewalk, coming on midnight, a lull in their conversation prolonged itself into an uncomfortable silence.

"So what comes next, Fang?" she asked, curiosity and the courage afforded by wine blended as one.

"What do you mean?" he said.

"I mean, when you get better. Are you going to fight again?"

"Yes," he said.

"And what about us – you and I, I mean."

"We keep seeing each other. Nothing changes."

"I would love that," she said. There was still the slightest hint of uncertainty, but it was gone after a pause.

The walk home took longer, both stumbling slightly, passing a borrowed bottle of wine back and forth. The stars were out, the cloudless day having turned to cloudless night. The moon was new, nearly absent. Fang pointed out several constellations to her, cradling her against him as they grew nearer to Lo Yan.

As they came to the street parallel to the

walled city, Fang paused, reeling slightly. He leaned against a nearby street sign, then pulled a cigarette from his pocket.

"I thought you'd quit," she said.

"Not yet. Too soon," Fang replied, smoke bouncing between his lips. He found his matchbox, struck a match, and lit the end. He took a deep haul, then blew it out heavily.

"Why'd we stop?" she swayed on her feet. The booze was going to her head. She needed to lie down next to Fang, to run her hand over his chest, to feel his hands run over her.

"Just a moment. Just to see something." Fang squinted, but nothing changed.

She didn't say anything, still swaying to the beat of an invisible tune. She took another swig from the bottle, the warmth of the red flooding down her throat.

Police sirens shattered their moment, and then Fang was once again with her. His eyes never left the rooftops, though, as if he were searching for something.

"Nothing. Nothing at all. Nothing changes. Nothing will change," he said to himself.

He looped his arm about hers, and together they stumbled through the mouth of Lo Yan. Through the bleak labyrinth, a city of two, the walls crumbling about them.

Acknowledgements

My personal thanks go out to my beta readers: Rachel Anderson, Gene Mercer, Krista Vaughan, and Jenny Trites. I'd also like to thank my parents for providing a childhood filled with '80s action flicks and martial arts movies as well as instilling a love of reading and writing. Of course, Mr. Reynolds is to be commended for his assistance in cleaning up the manuscript.

Problematic Press is a small, independent book publishing endeavour based in St. John's, NL. Problematic Press has a mission with a broad scope, aiming to entertain and educate readers of all ages.

Perhaps that's problematic. Problems make us think.

http://problematicpress.wordpress.com

James De Mille's *A Strange Manuscript Found in a Copper Cylinder* is one of the first Canadian texts to explore science fiction. 125 years after its release, this tale is still sure to thrill and excite audiences!

Vester Vade Mecum: A Collection of Short Fiction includes works by such authors as Washington Irving, Edgar Allan Poe, Mary Shelley, Oscar Wilde, Arthur Conan Doyle, Pauline Hopkins, plus others! This anthology revisits many classic tales that remain surprisingly relevant today. Enjoy!

Made in United States
Troutdale, OR
08/15/2023

12107260R00163